THE GIFTED COMPLEX

Book 1 of The Gifted World Series

L. D. Valencia

Thanks for being awesome.

Copyright © 2020 L. D. Valencia

*All Rights Reserved. No part of this publication may be reproduced
in any form or by any means, including scanning, photocopying,
or otherwise without prior written permission of the copyright holder.*

First Printing, 2020

Printed in the United States of America

CONTENTS

PROLOGUE

EDEN

On a cool morning in early spring, a young boy stirred in his sleep as an alarm clock blared from a nightstand to his left. He reached to silence it. However, it was just out of reach. Once again he reached, but still nothing. Then he threw out his hand, accidently sending the alarm clock flying off the nightstand. However, he never made contact with it. Once again, he'd used his *gift* a little too forcefully.

He sat up and swung his legs down to reach the floor. The hair on his legs sprang up, and a shiver ran through him. The cool wood floor was at the same time jolting and refreshing.

He closed his eyes and sighed. *Now to get ready for the big day,* he thought. He stood up and let out a tremendous yawn. With a stretch to the left and a turn to the right, he felt ready to begin the day.

He passed a dresser with a soccer ball covered in signatures. Then he stepped over a pair of cleats on his way to the bathroom. In the bathroom, he looked into the mirror. His gray eyes peered at his reflection. His brown hair was a mess as it usually was in the morning. Gabriel wasn't sure how, but when he woke up his hair was always as messy as possible.

He had to look "presentable." as his mother said. Today was an important day. In his closet, he grabbed his favorite white button-down shirt with a blue-striped pattern. Once dressed, the young man ran downstairs for a quick breakfast. His soccer coaches always told him to eat as healthy as possible for breakfast. So as usual, he made a bowl of an organic cereal, pouring two-percent milk overtop of it.

Afterward, he sat on his living room couch, rocking back and forth, waiting for the recruiter to arrive. His parents were in the kitchen, preparing some refreshments for their guest. Despite the tranquil mood in his house, he couldn't fight the anxious torrent inside of him. He played a good part, pretending to be calm. However, he felt like a storm was raging inside his mind.

***

Outside the house, a car pulled up and parked on the curb. It wasn't a terribly nice car, but it got the job done. The man inside put the car into park. He was about to get out of the car when his phone went off. He answered his device, and instantly his heart jumped. His pulse raced the way it does when someone really important compliments you.

"Morning, sir," he answered.

The voice over the phone spoke for a moment.

"Yes, I am concerned as well," the man answered.

Once again the voice on the other end spoke.

"Yes, yes, sir. I understand the situation we are in."

Once again, the voice over the phone asked him a question.

"Well, I am about to go into a meeting with a young man that I feel has great potential. He's shown amazing aptitude on our entrance exams, and he has a very rare and powerful gift."

The voice on the other line asked another question.

"Well, it's telekinesis."

He waited for a moment for the voice to speak.

"Well sir, you understand my gift. I just have a feeling, an instinctive feeling that this boy is special. I think he will be important to our organization."

***

Back inside, Gabriel found himself daydreaming. Then a knock at the door snapped him back to reality. He stood up, straightened out his shirt, and then walked over to the door. When he opened it, the light beamed in behind the man at the front door. A middle-aged man stood there. But Gabriel could barely see him as the sunshine was so bright.

"Hello, is Gabriel Green home?" he asked.

The boy nods his head and says, "Yes, that is me, sir."

"I see you have gray eyes," stated the man. Gabriel looked up to meet his eyes, but the man was wearing a baseball cap so low it was almost hard to see his eyes. The hat had a school logo upon it. Gabriel noticed his salt-and-pepper hair sticking out of the sides. The front of the navy-blue hat had the letters *SIA* embroidered in red.

"Yes, sir," replied Gabriel.

"Do you know why?"

"Well, because I was born with them," answered Gabriel. "Sir," he added after a slight pause.

The man smirked and let out a chuckle. Then he said, "Well, I supposed that isn't the wrong answer, now is it?"

Gabriel had never realized that before. He hadn't thought about it too much. His eyes were just the color they were. But now that he thought about it, no one else he knew had eyes the same color as his. Out of all of his classmates, Gabe was the only one with this unique quality.

With that, the man stepped inside. Then they made their way to the living room and sat silently for a few seconds. The man introduced himself as Coach V, teacher and coach at SIA. He began by asking the boy about himself and what his personal interests were. Gabriel mentioned he would be trying out for the soccer team now that he was in high school.

After some time, Coach V got out his checklist. He pulled out a pen from his shirt pocket and some forms from his briefcase. It had several things he needed to get some personal information about Gabriel. "So, name, Gabriel Green. Check," he said, writing down Gabriel's name in the first blank. "Next, I need to see your gift, your ability. Just for confirmation."

Gabriel glanced at the floor and then at the coffee table between Coach V and himself. He focused his eyes on it. They turned a silvery color for a second. Instantly, the table began to lift in the air. The papers on the table all floated off the coffee table into the air as well. After a few seconds of levitating, they began to shake. Then they dropped to the ground with a loud thump.

Coach instantly noticed the strained look on Gabriel's face. A thin layer of sweat was beginning to form on Gabriel's forehead. Coach stared into Gabriel's eyes. "Hmm, is it hard to control?" he asked.

"Yes. Sometimes, but it also gives me headaches."

Then Coach V handed Gabriel a business card. Gabriel thumbed the edges of the card stock. Then he looked down and read:

Coach V

SIA Athletic Director and sparring team Coach

Office Hours Monday–Friday 3:00 p.m. through 6:00 p.m.

Then at the bottom it had a phone number. Coach V pointed his finger on the number. "This is my school number. Call me anytime you feel you need advice or help with your ability."

Gabe nodded and said, "Thank you! I will!"

The coach stood up. He walked around the room and looked at the pictures of Gabriel and his family on the wall. His baby pictures, his school photos. His eyes saw a class photo with Gabriel from fourth grade. Gabe stood in the very center of the photo. A thought crossed Coach's mind.

"Do you feel unusual at school, Gabriel?" asked Coach V.

"Well, sometimes. Most of the kids in my school are pretty nice about it. There are a few bullies that make a point of teasing me about my differences."

"That is to be expected," Coach replied. "Don't let that get you down, Gabriel. You have a lot to be proud of and don't let anyone tell you differently."

"Thank you," answered Gabriel.

Coach looked down at his files. "With the rarity of your gift and your good grades, we would likely be able to get you a full scholarship to our school."

"The school with people with eyes like mine, you mean?" asked Gabriel.

Gabriel smiled, thinking his comment was humorous. However, Coach V smirked briefly and then returned to his files. Coach didn't seem to be the sort to joke around at all.

The coach replied, "Yes, but our college is a college like any other. We accept gifted and nongifted students. The thing that makes our school different than most, is that we have a gifted department. Not a lot of schools do. But we want to make sure that when students with gifts leave our school, they will use their gift to make the world safer, stronger, and better than they found it."

Instantly, Gabriel felt an intense draw to the school. The idea that he would be with students that would accept him as he was made him eager to attend. Not only that, but also he would be able to learn how to better control his telekinesis. No more headaches when he tried to use his telekinesis.

"So, Gabriel, would you like that?" asked the coach.

"Yes, sir, I would very much," Gabe answered. "When can I start?"

Coach V sat back down and pulled up his briefcase. He set it down on the coffee table in between Gabriel and him. He placed it flat against the espresso-colored wood.

Coach V stated, "Well, you need to finish high school first."

He continued to undo the straps on his briefcase. He reached his hand inside and pulled out a stack of documents. Placing them on the coffee table between Gabe and himself, Coach V grabbed a pen from his pocket and clicked it open.

"But after finishing at SIA, you can go to any other school you want if you want to get your degree in something else. Some students want to pursue more advanced degrees to future their contributions to the world."

"Ready to sign up?" asked Coach V.

Gabriel eagerly held out his hand. Coach V grabbed his hand and shook it firmly confirming their agreement.

Then Coach V's facial expression became very different. His expression turned much more serious, and his eyes became very steady. Gabriel looked at him and noticed the somber expression on his face.

"Sir? What's wrong?" asked Gabriel.

"Before you sign that. I have something I want to ask you," stated Coach V. "Can you answer this question for me?"

"Yes. I mean, I will do my best."

"Thank you," answered Coach V. "Most people don't know that the world is in a very fragile state right now. Gifted are seen in a positive light right now. But there are forces that are moving against us, even as we speak. We need more gifted such as yourself—ones who are willing to help make this world a better place."

As the coach spoke, his eyes became filled with what Gabriel could only explain as fire. As he spoke, Gabriel nodded his head in agreement.

"Can you be someone who will stand up against adversity and fight for truth?" asked Coach V with a look filled with determination.

The young man sat across the table, his hands folded in his lap. His heart was racing from the words spoken by Coach V. Never had he heard a speech that had caused everything inside of him to be so fired up. He felt as if something in his bones was sparking. It was as if electricity had shot through his entire body. Gabe's head looked up from the wooden coffee table where the forms were laying.

Just before Gabriel could answer, his mother walked in with a tray of food in her hands. Gabriel's father walked in behind her. They were both all smiles.

His mother nodded her head and said, "Lunch is ready, gentlemen. Come on in."

Coach V stood up from his seat, and Gabriel did likewise. Their eyes were locked for a moment. Coach turned to walk into the dining room, but Gabe stopped him to say, "Yes, sir." Coach looked back at Gabriel.

"I want to be that kind of person," he answered.

FILE #1

CRASH LANDING

The excitement of the day was apparent in the room—high energy and full of potential. A young boy rushed from corner to corner of the room, throwing the last few objects into bags sitting at the door of his bedroom. It was a normal boy's room. Sports posters lined the walls. The paint was a dark blue that appeared lighter as the morning sunlight broke through the curtains.

Today was a big day—the day Gabriel went to the campus of SIA, his college. Everything was almost ready. His filled bags finally stood at the door of his room. The room had been removed of all the essentials—his toothbrush, clothes, and phone, all the things a normal teenager would need for going to college.

However, Gabriel wasn't a normal teenager going to college. He would be attending Sabot Institute of America, one of the few colleges in the country that had a gifted department. He paused and pulled the brochure out again, still in disbelief. In one hand he held the acceptance letter and in the other the brochure he'd received a few weeks ago. The brochure said *Sabot Institute of America* along the front in bright-red letters over a field of navy blue. He scanned the headings.

Several catchphrases—*Control your Gift, Enrich the World,* and *Improve the Lives of Millions*—covered the inside of the brochure. He opened it up. Over to the left was a checklist of all the things to bring when coming to the campus. A few were ones that Gabriel almost forgot to grab. Most were the essentials he'd packed last weekend. But he scanned the rest to make sure he was ready. He had his paperwork in his bag, a list of classes he wanted, and a form he'd filled out with his parents to take care of enrolling for classes.

Stopping in the doorway, Gabriel took one last look around his room. "See you in a few months," he said and closed the door. Then Gabriel went to meet his parents downstairs. From the bottom of the stairs, he could hear his mother humming in the kitchen. He walked to the front door and peeked outside. It was a warm August day, and Gabriel could see his neighbors across the street. Mr. Duran was mowing his lawn with a red push mower, and his wife was weeding her garden.

A large garbage truck was rolling down the road, stopping at each house on the block. It stopped at his next-door neighbor's house and came to a grinding halt. Then Gabriel heard a grizzled voice grunting. He looked around the corner and spotted his father. He was carrying a large box labeled *Gabriel's Stuff* down the side, going to place it into the back of their SUV.

Gabriel hopped from the stairs and yelled, "Wait. Let me do it!"

"Why?" his father asked, confused.

Excitedly, Gabriel answered. "Here, let me show you how much better I have gotten with my telekinesis."

Gabriel held out his hand and lifted the first box into the air. Using his hand as a guide, like a marksman uses a sight to aim, he carefully pushed the box in between two others in the back of their car. He repeated the process with the next, much larger box. It shook slightly as he lifted it up and into the vehicle, but he was able to make it without dropping anything. Not like last time.

"Not perfect, but better, right?" Gabriel asked his father.

"Glad to see you're learning to use your power so well."

Just then, Gabriel's mother stepped onto the porch. "Very nicely done, Gabe," she said.

Gabriel and his father moved all of the boxes into the trunk. As Gabriel lifted the last box with his mind, he felt a sudden twinge of pain between his eyes. He blinked his eyes rapidly in an attempt to stop the pain. But it quickly increased and suddenly became a screaming jolt of agony completely crippling him. Before he could even think, he dropped to one knee, holding his scalp.

In a panic, Mrs. Green rushed to her son. "Are you all right, Gabe?" she asked with concern in her voice.

Gabriel's father moved to check on his son as well. Realizing his son's discomfort, he knelt down beside Gabriel. When Gabriel opened his eyes, the first thing he saw was the salt-and-pepper color of his father's hair. His eyes were intense and focused. Gabriel noticed the deep brown of his irises and the age lines around his brow. The dark stubble on his face showed he hadn't shaved this morning. Although much more tan, Gabriel's father looked like a grown-up version of Gabe.

"Are you feeling all right?" he asked his son.

Gabriel held up his hand and said, "It's just a headache."

"You haven't had one of those in a long time," his dad said.

"Not since last year," Gabriel said shortly. He paused for a moment. After a few deep breaths, he continued. "It has been a while, but one was bound to show up eventually."

Gabriel's mom raised her soft, pale hands to Gabriel's head. She placed a hand on each of Gabriel's temples. Her touch was firm but gentle. Slowly, she massaged his temples in a circular fashion. After a few minutes, Gabriel could tell the headache was fading.

He stood up, and his mother pressed him to her, hugging him tightly. She whispered, "All better?" in his ear.

He nodded.

"Why don't you take a break and get some breakfast?" his father said.

Gabriel gripped his skull, driving his fingers into his skin. The pain was all but gone, but a light-headed feeling still remained. "All right," Gabriel answered.

Inside, his mother handed Gabriel a clear glass of water. "Drink up," she said softly. Her calming voice helped sooth his nerves like a medicine.

"You know what your gift is, Mom?" Gabriel asked.

"I don't have a gift, Gabe. You know that."

"Yes, you do. Comfort and compassion. Plus, you are the best nurse ever."

His mother laughed. "That's just what I've learned from being in the medical field for twenty years. Nothing super about it at all."

After a large gulp of water, Gabriel replied, "What? You make people better. You help them heal and give them hope."

"If you say so. But you're the one who is really gifted."

Gabriel's head dropped. "If you ask me, people like you are really the gifted ones. You do amazing things every day."

Gabriel unwrapped a granola bar and quickly chewed it up. Meanwhile, his mother stood in the kitchen almost in tears from her son's kind words. "I'll miss you, Gabriel."

Before Gabriel could answer, his father stepped into the room. "All ready to go," he said, looking at his watch. It was a beaten old watch, one with multiple functions. He preferred it to the fancier watch his family bought him because of its practicality. He tapped the watch twice in a motion to hurry the family.

Gabriel's little sister was at the kitchen table, coloring her picture of a princess riding a unicorn. Her soft auburn hair caught a glint of sunlight in the window, highlighting the reds in her hair. Gabriel picked her up, and she squealed in excitement. "Let's go, Princess Leigh!" he said.

The family crammed into the vehicle and were off. Sitting in his seat, Gabriel looked over at his little sister. Her laughter was contagious. It caused a smile to instantly form on his face. She giggled as she played with two dolls in her lap, sitting in her gray booster seat. Her smile warmed his heart. He wanted to savor the moment, knowing that he wouldn't be seeing her for some time. Gabriel's sister was a miracle, and something about the fact that she had almost been lost to them made their connection that much stronger.

He remembered the day she'd been born. There had been a complication—something about the umbilical cord being wrapped around her neck. It had been startling news for both the parents and Gabriel. People don't think of a birth being a time of terror, but the doctors had worked for several hours. Gabriel had sat in the waiting room with his grandparents, Andy and Diane. They had been the most calming part of that day—sitting with him, encouraging him, and praying with him while he waited.

Finally, his father and a doctor had emerged from the operating room. They had shaken hands, and then his father had walked over to them in the waiting room. With a look of relief on his face, Mr. Green had spoken softly. "She's here."

Gabriel had run to his father, who was wearing a matching pair of doctor's scrubs and a mask over his chin. The day had been wearing on everyone, but in the end Leigh had been born happy and healthy. Gabriel wasn't sure if she knew it, but something had changed in Gabriel that day. He'd changed down to his very core. No longer was he the only child. It was as if all of the selfishness was wrenched out of him like a damp towel being twisted dry.

Gabriel knew how special this little girl was, and the thought of almost losing her on the day he was going to meet her made him realize how special life was. Gabriel had been a new person that day. Leigh would have a permanent condition after her near-fatal birth, but that had only made her more special to Gabriel.

Gabriel looked at her in the seat across from him. Then he noticed a sign outside her window. They were still pretty far away. The drive was not a long one. Before long, they were nearing the campus of SIA, and Gabriel could see the sign for the campus on the highway. His heart began to beat with excitement. He could feel the rush of his heart in his legs, it was so extreme. They pulled off at their exit and onto a smaller road. It was called Academic Drive, and Gabriel knew this road led to the campus. After a few minutes, they came to a stoplight.

Gabriel's father turned back and looked at Gabriel. "We're almost there. Are you excited?" he asked Gabriel.

"You know it," answered Gabriel excitedly.

The light turned green, and they pulled forward. Gabriel looked out his window, hoping to see the school campus in the distance. However, just as he looked out, he saw something much different. A large black truck was driving right at them. In that split second, Gabriel could see the driver's face; he wasn't looking at the road. Just then the driver realized his error and slammed on the brakes. It wouldn't matter. It was too late. Within a second the truck would be smashing into them.

Without thinking, Gabriel threw up his hands to shield himself—natural self-defense in such a time. However, it would not be enough to save him. But without realizing it, Gabriel's telekinetic energy shielded the car. The large vehicle smashed into their car, inches from Gabriel.

Normally, the force of a truck that size would break through an SUV. However, somehow the telekinetic shield protected them from the truck. Instead of smashing through the car, the truck pushed the Green's SUV through the intersection into the adjacent road. The force was so great that the wheels left large black streaks on the pavement.

Afterward, the entire family was frozen in place. A cold air of shock gripped all of them. Nobody moved for several seconds. It all happened so fast that no one was quite sure exactly what had just happened. But Gabriel began to feel fuzzy. Gabriel's mother turned and looked back at Gabriel and

Leigh. They were completely uninjured. Her eyes fixed on Gabriel after making sure Leigh was completely unharmed. She saw his face was covered in a mask of pain. He was sweating. He had the same expression as when he got those intense headaches.

"What just happened?" his father asked from the driver side.

"I ... I ..." Gabriel tried to answer. But before he could come up with more than that, everything went dark.

***

He awoke an hour later on a stretcher in an ambulance. His little sister, Leigh, was gripping his hand fiercely. She was asleep, sitting with her head resting on his side. He stirred and then sat up. Everything was white. He saw a clear mask was attached to his face, giving him oxygen to breathe. He pulled it off and coughed as the scent of smoke was still in the air. He looked over at the scene.

A black truck was in the intersection where their SUV was hit. It was smashed in on the front. The vehicle was missing most of the hood, and the bumper was gone. Gabriel moved to get up, and his sister awoke from her sleep. He focused back on the truck. It looked like it was totaled.

Leigh whispered something, but Gabriel was so enthralled by what he was seeing that he didn't catch it. He stood and exited the back of the ambulance. Standing on the pavement, he could see it. Their SUV was completely unharmed. It had left a rubber skid mark where it had been pushed along the asphalt road. But other than that, the car was fine. It had moved from where it had originally been hit, but the black streaks showed the scene of the accident.

Gabriel looked around. His head shooting from the left to the right. "Where are my parents?" he whispered through a raspy voice.

Immediately an emergency medical technician recognized him and came rushing over to him.

Gabriel was shaking. "Where are my parents?" he begged.

"Your parents are fine. They are being looked at by another EMT," she said to him in her calmest voice. "You are in shock. Can you tell me your name?"

"Gabriel, Gabriel Green," he said through the stuttering. "Can I see my dad?"

The EMT brought Gabriel over to the ambulance that housed his parents. His mother was inside the back of the vehicle, but his father was sitting on the back bumper. Once he saw Gabriel, he instantly stood up and rushed over to him. Before Gabriel could even think, he was being wrapped by two burly arms that squeezed him tightly. His embrace was powerful. He gripped Gabriel as if he'd been gone for ages. But it was more than that; this was a hug that said thank you.

His father pulled back and looked at Gabriel intensely. Unsure of what he was looking at, Gabriel looked back confused.

"You wonderful, wonderful kid," his father said with a tone of appreciation.

"Gabriel," his mother yelled and hopped down from the back of the ambulance to reach him. She flung herself onto them and grabbed them with all her might. Then Gabe felt a pressure on his leg. He looked down and saw the top of Leigh's head. She was wrapped around his left leg, hugging him tightly.

"What happened?" he asked completely unsure of what was going on.

"The driver was not watching the road apparently," his dad said. Then pointing to the crash scene, he said, "Then that happened."

The EMT walked over. A policeman was standing beside her. He held his hat in his hands and had a digital tablet under his right arm. He had a calm demeanor, but his expression was all business. "Hello, Mr. and Mrs. Green. Is this the boy? The gifted?"

His father let them go from their hug and turned to face the officer. "Yes, sir."

"Son," he said looking at Gabriel. "I don't believe your family would have survived that crash if it wasn't for you. Somehow you protected them with your gift." He paused for a moment, possibly to let the news sink in. "I guess that's why they call them gifts."

Gabriel looked over to the SUV. "Is the car still drivable?" he asked. "We need to get to school."

His father wrapped an arm around him and kissed his head. "Don't you realize what this man is telling you, Gabriel? You're a hero. You saved your mother, your sister, and me."

The brown hair of Gabriel's head was in a mess as he combed his hand through it. He didn't know what to say.

The policeman stepped forward. "You're going to be staying the night in town. We would like to get your statement for the report before we let you on your way. Where were you headed again?"

"Saboth Institute of America," Gabriel stated. "Will we be late?"

"SIA," the officer state. "That makes sense since you are a gifted. Well, the report should be done tonight, and you can be off first thing in the morning."

Gabriel shot a look at his mother. She was the strict one. She never let Gabriel be late for anything. He was sure she would insist that the officer finish his report now and let them get going soon. But she looked at him, and her expression softened.

In a voice that was barely a whisper, she said, "We will be fine if we get there tomorrow morning. You already have your room assignment, and we will call the school and let them know we had some car trouble."

Gabriel spent most of that afternoon speaking with police officers, insurance agencies, and doctors. The driver of the truck even approached Gabriel to apologize. He begged forgiveness, taking full responsibility for the accident.

"I couldn't have lived with myself if something happened to your family because of me."

Gabriel accepted his apology, but he wasn't sure how to reply. His anger swirled inside of him, but he gritted his teeth while the man spoke. His only answer was a head nod.

That night they stayed in a luxurious hotel down the road from the campus. Gabriel could see the tall tower of one of the buildings from his room. He spent the evening lost in thought, wondering what this semester would have in store for him.

"There's no way it can get any crazier than today," said Gabriel to himself.

FILE #2

ROOMMATES

The following morning a rental car was waiting for Gabriel as he stepped out of the hotel. Although their car was completely unharmed, the insurance company insisted they take a rented SUV while theirs was looked at by a mechanic. His father accepted the keys from the attendant and nodded politely. The gentleman was in a dark black suit and gray tie. He held the door open for Gabriel's mother, and she entered the vehicle. Meanwhile, Gabriel helped his sister get into her car seat and buckle in. The man even loaded the boxes into the car for them.

Before long they were entering the campus. The hotel was just up the road from the campus. Gabriel was certain many parents stayed there as they helped get their children settled in for college life. Some parents couldn't let their children go. Gabriel was glad his parents weren't the overly clingy type. He remembered his mother telling him about his first day of kindergarten. When Gabriel had exited the car, his mother had wanted to walk him inside. But Gabriel stood there and said, "No, Mom. I'm a big boy, and I have a lot of things to do today."

On campus, swarms of people were walking all over the place. Parents, grandparents, aunts, uncles, and of course students were everywhere. People were carrying boxes to their buildings. Students were standing in lines to order books and sign up for clubs. Gabriel decided he wanted to get settled in before signing up for anything.

Gabriel's father pulled to an intersection. A woman in a bright-red shirt stopped the Green's vehicle. "Can I help you all?" she said in an exceptionally perky voice.

"We are looking for the freshman dorm," his father stated as he skimmed an e-mail with direction for first day on campus.

"Here is a map," she said, handing him a folded piece of paper. "You will go down this street and then take a right at that stop sign." She pointed out the directions to him.

His father accelerated and drove in that direction. He came to a stop at the sign and waited for a large group of pedestrians to cross the street. They were all walking in the same direction. Then Gabriel saw where they were going—a massive brick building. Over the archway a massive stone slab in the wall had the words "Ion Dormitory" carved into it. This was the freshman dorm building.

They took that right-hand turn and found themselves in a large parking lot. Somehow his father could sense an open parking spot. Gabriel called it "his gift." But this was a joke, of course. Gabriel knew his father had more to offer than just finding great parking spots. His father was a police officer in Jericho, the largest city in eastern Pennsylvania. Gabriel admired people like his father, who laid down their lives for the people they served. It was a note of pride with Gabriel that his parents had the kind of jobs that worked to help people. He knew he wanted to do the same.

Quickly, they found a spot and pulled in right outside of the dorm building. Gabriel was the first one out of the car. He ran around the side of the car and stared up at the building. The stone bricks gleamed in the sunlight. He remembered the first time he'd seen this building, last summer when his family had toured the campus before officially deciding to attend.

Gabriel looked out at all the crowds. He thought, *You can't tell who's gifted and who's not. We are all the same.* As he looked around, he smiled at all of the students. Gabriel was certain that coming to this school and getting into the gifted department would help him become the man he wanted to be.

Gabriel grabbed a few boxes from the back of the new SUV. As he did so he thought how fortunate it was that most of his boxes were filled with clothes, bedding, and school supplies. They weren't filled with anything majorly breakable.

His mother just then rounded the corner of the vehicle and asked. "Why don't you head in and meet your new roommate?"

He nodded in reply. Then he turned and walked toward the building. He saw a mass of people inside the building and held his breath and dived in. Gabriel found the resident's assistant behind a desk at the entrance. He was a tall, burly boy much older than Gabriel. He held a clipboard in his hands as he checked off items on it. Gabriel gave the man his name and got his room assignment.

Gabriel found the stairs and made his way up to his room. He was glad he'd gotten an upstairs room, which had a better view of the skyline, he thought. However, it was harder to make it up the stairs than he'd anticipated. Several freshmen were doing the same thing that Gabriel was, pushing through the crowds going up and down the stairs. Most were carrying boxes like he was, and some were even bringing up furniture items like armchairs and lamps.

Coming up to the second floor, Gabriel began down the long hallway. On his left and right were rows of doors. Each had a number on it, all starting with a "2." Finally, he made his way to 209, his room. He came to the door, and it was opened. Inside he saw a boy standing at the window, unpacking a box. He had shoulder-length blond hair that was pulled into a messy sort of ponytail. He wore a red sleeveless shirt and shorts that showed his lightly tanned skin.

"Are you the other guy?" the boy asked excitedly, but then his face fell and he quickly seemed to pull back.

Immediately Gabriel was taken aback by the boy's response. He wasn't sure if this was an insult or not. "If you mean, 'Am I your roommate?' then yes," Gabriel answered in a less-than-enthused voice.

The other boy apologized. "I'm sorry. I meant, are you my roommate? That came out kind of wrong." He held out his hand and shook Gabriel's, meeting him at the door. "I'm Jake Burns. Nice to meet you."

"Gabriel Green," Gabriel answered, shaking Jake's hand.

"Sometimes I say things without thinking," said Jake in an apologetic way. "I didn't want to seem too eager."

The boys sized each other up for a moment. Each of them tried to remain cool and collected. They put on a nonchalant attitude, so they would come across as unimpressed. There was an awkward silence that lasted several seconds.

Gabriel pretended to look around the room. He knew what the room looked like from his tours, but he was actually sizing up Jake. Gabriel thought he must be a student athlete, possibly on the baseball team. His height was average, slim, and lean.

Meanwhile, Jake looked back at Gabriel. He saw an average height guy with brown hair. His eyes were silver, which Jake found interesting as his eyes were gold. Gabriel wore a pair of jeans and sneakers. From what Jake could tell, he was a cool guy.

Just then Gabriel's parents came up. His father had a stack of boxes in his arms. His mother, however, only had her purse and a small box. Leigh trailed behind them carrying her princess and unicorn dolls, asking her mother if Gabriel was in trouble for needing to go to a special school.

"Hello, I'm Mr. Green. Nice to meet you," said Gabe's father, shaking Jake's hand.

"And I'm Mrs. Green," she said with a smile. "This is Leigh, our daughter." Leigh did a twirl and bowed, making a big show of it.

Jake greeted them politely. "It's totally great to meet you all. I'm Jake Burns."

They perused the room. It was a small all-in-one room. The kitchen, living room, and bedrooms were all in one big, open space. From the door where they stood, the kitchen was on their right and the living room was on the left. The "bedroom," if you could call it that, was just the far wall where two beds stayed on opposite corners. Two small desks were beside each of the beds with some papers that said, "Welcome to SIA," across the front.

"The room is smaller than I remembered," stated Mrs. Green.

Mr. Green laughed. "Well, next year he'll get a bigger room. Freshman dorms are always the smallest."

Gabriel nodded in agreement. "It's fine," he said with a tone of appreciation. "I'm sure we will be out doing stuff most of the time anyway."

***

Gabriel was bringing up the last of his boxes as Jake was unpacking. When he entered the room, Jake was laying things down on the bed to the right. "I'm already set up over here," he said, looking at Gabriel to gauge whether that was fine with him.

Gabriel answered back with a sigh, "Yeah, that's fine with me."

He walked toward the bed on the left. They each were identical, so Gabriel didn't mind too much. He saw the sun setting out the window. From this spot, Gabriel admired the beauty of the sun. It was painting yellows and pinks on the clouds as it set behind them. The sky was a mesmerizing splash of colors.

After helping him set up a little, Gabriel's parents said their farewells. Unfortunately, they couldn't stay long. His father had a meeting to attend back in the city, and they had remained in the area longer than expected. His mother gave him a big kiss, leaving red lipstick on his cheek. Gabe's father slapped him once on the back and said, "I expect you to be on the dean's list," in his joking but stern voice.

Gabe laughed, holding his back, which was now throbbing. "I will, Dad, no worries." Gabriel's father didn't seem to know his own strength. That or his slaps on the back were intentionally painful.

Leigh hugged Gabriel so tightly he thought she might never let go. Her face was red, and small tears cascaded down her face. "I love you, Gabey."

"I love you too, Leigh."

***

After they left, it took Gabriel about an hour to finish unpacking the rest of his things. He didn't get to decorating or arranging anything, because his stomach began to growl with ferocious hunger. He sat on his bed and looked over to Jake. "Want to eat?" Gabe asked.

Jake declined, saying that he already had eaten before Gabe had arrived. Gabriel decided to make a quick sandwich with the groceries his mother had left in the fridge.

Just before nightfall, Gabriel finished setting up. Jake had finished and was sitting on the couch in the living room area. The whole room was one big rectangle, and everything was visible except for the bathroom, which was its own room.

Jake arose from the couch and flipped off the small television set. He walked over to his bed. Then stopped in the middle of the room. He went to the restroom and washed up for bed. When he exited, he looked out at Gabriel and leaned on the doorframe. "Hey, orientation is tomorrow morning. Do you want to go?"

"Sure," answered Gabriel.

"Excellent," he said. Then he shrugged like he didn't care. Gabriel could tell he was just trying to act aloof and macho.

***

The following morning, Gabriel dressed and met Jake outside for orientation. Jake had slept in, so Gabriel waited downstairs since he was excited to get going. Today they would hear from the school administration. Orientation was like a welcome to the newcomers to the institute.

Outside, Gabriel was zipping up his hoodie to combat the cool morning air. Fall was coming early, it seemed, because that morning was a brisk and cool temperature. When Gabriel saw Jake come down with a tank top and shorts outfit, he was a little surprised.

"How are you dressed like that?" demanded Gabriel, completely bewildered.

"It's a side effect of my gift," answered Jake.

Gabriel just realized that he hadn't even asked, so immediately correcting that problem, he asked, "What's your gift?"

"Pyrokinesis. I can control fire."

"Cool, can you show me?" Gabe asked excitedly.

"Hmm, so you see, I am not very good at making fire out of the air like some can. But I am really good at manipulating it."

Jake pulled a small object from his pocket. It was black as night and had rough edges. It looked like it was metal, but it was so dark it was hard to tell.

"Do you usually keep metal in your pocket?" asked Gabe, thinking he was being funny.

"It's flint. It's used to create sparks for a fire. And yes, yes, I do," Jake answered. Then he winked. "You never know when you will need to impress a cute girl."

Then Jake bent down and struck it against the ground. It made a small spark. But instantly that spark burst into a small flame. Jake made the flame jump up into his hand, and then it expanded rapidly. The small ball of fire bounced between his hands like a tennis ball. Then he caught it in his left hand and held it out to show Gabriel.

Gabriel jumped back, alarmed at the fire burning Jake's hands. But Jake stopped him, waving his other hand.

"It's ok. I'm all right. See?"

Gabe looked on in amazement. He put his hand closer to the flame and felt the heat. "Wow, you can touch fire and not be burned?"

"Yeah, like I said, it's a neat side effect. I don't really notice heat at all. Plus, cold weather doesn't even bother me."

"Wow!" Gabe announced in amazement.

"Yeah, it's like there is this flame inside of me all the time. Makes me really warm-natured."

"That is a nice gift to have when it is this cold out."

"Yeah, but the downside is that I don't really notice warmth, because I am always hot. You know?" Jake answered, shrugging his shoulders.

The two began walking down the path to the main walkway, known as the Quad. The Quad was in the center of the university, and all of the main buildings were on the Quad, such as the Student Union Building, which everyone called the Sub. And most of the main lecture halls were along the Quad as well.

When they arrived at the Quad, Jake was impressed at the scope of the buildings. Huge, towering structures and massive brickwork made the Quad an interesting sight. The center was several ornate pieces of cement arranged in a unique pattern. Looking down, Jake realized that the slabs were all counties in the state. It was a giant map of Pennsylvania made out of cement.

Gabe saw booths inside the Sub. "Let's go check it out!"

Inside the Quad, there were rows of tables with signs taped to them advertising various school club names. All the different groups were holding sign-ups for their clubs. The entire foyer was swarming with students signing up for different clubs, teams, or activities. There were musicians playing music in one corner, a group of comic book collectors debating trivia near the doorway, and a pack of jocks guarded the workout area. All in all, the entire room was packed.

Gabriel thought it would be fun to see the different clubs and maybe even join one.

Gabriel looked at Jake. "Are you going to join a club?"

"Well, I was accepted into the sparring team. Bu—" Jake was unable to finish as Gabriel interjected.

"You're on the sparring team?" Gabriel asked excitedly.

"Technically, yeah, but I haven't practiced yet. Why?"

"I was thinking about joining it. But I heard it is pretty dangerous."

Jake answered back. "Yeah, supposedly it can be. But I have heard amazing things about Coach V. He said he can help me figure out with my fire-generation issue."

They continued to walk down the center. Then Jake noticed a booth that could be interesting. The stand was blue, with a banner painted in the school colors, navy blue and a deep red. It was painted in a glossy paint that gave it a shiny look with the overhead lights. In big red letters it read, "sports club."

Jake looked intrigued, while Gabriel walked right past. "I am probably going to join the sports club as well," Jake stated bluntly. "What about you?"

Gabriel paused and turned around. He strolled nonchalantly back toward Jake and looked at the booth. In a cavalier tone he answered, "I could get into that too."

"Oh, so you like sports too?" Jake asked.

"Yeah, I played on my football team in high school, and I've played soccer since I was a kid."

"Cool. I was on the track and wrestling teams from middle school into high school."

Gabriel was not surprised. Jake looked like he'd started lifting weights when he'd been an infant. His muscles were much more defined than Gabriel's. He had a lean frame, but his biceps were much thicker than a normal person his size.

"Where did you go to school?" asked Gabriel, the thought just popping into his head.

Jake sighed deeply for a moment and then answered, "Here and there. We moved a lot because of my dad's job. So I was in a lot of different schools. And you?"

"Born and raised in Bethlehem, Pennsylvania, not too far from here."

Gabe and Jake got in line for the sports club. Gabriel didn't know if he had time to play much, but he was assured by Jake that it wasn't attendance based.

Once the person in front of them was finished, Gabriel stepped forward and grabbed an application. Jake did likewise. Gabriel filled in his information. He barely had to even read the form, as it mirrored all of the other forms he'd filled out for school.

At the bottom, it asked for any medical issues that might hinder him in a sport. Gabriel looked over to make sure Jake wasn't looking. Once he felt he was safe, Gabe wrote, "I used to have asthma, but my condition isn't serious."

Jake looked over his shoulder and saw Gabriel's form. "You have asthma?" he asked, causing Gabriel to feel a small tinge of shame.

Gabriel dropped his head for a moment. He had been hoping to avoid anyone seeing that. Although he knew it wasn't a bad thing, it was always something he felt sensitive about. But since it had been made known, he had no choice but to answer.

"No, not really. Well, kinda. But it is really not a big deal. I guess it worked because I haven't even used my inhaler since I was in middle school. I don't even keep it with me anymore."

Jake patted Gabriel on the back. "It's no big deal, man," Jake said reassuringly. "But that's good to hear."

Then handed his form to the scrappy young man at the booth. He was tall and lanky, but had a solid build. He wore gym shorts and a bright yellow T-shirt with the generic workout phrase, *No Pain, No Gain*. He told the boys that the club played a sport a few times a month, more once it got warmer, but while it was cold, they would stick to indoor sports. However, the other clubs also liked to use the indoor fields whenever possible, which made playing sports in the early winter harder.

"Our first game will be Saturday night of this week, okay?" he stated energetically. "We are playing indoor soccer."

Gabriel shot him a look that showed his enthusiasm. "Great," he exclaimed.

Gabriel turned from the booth and saw a striking figure. He angled his head to get a better view of the pretty redhead across the Quad. Gabriel took a step to the right and watched her. She wore a scarf around her neck and a jean jacket over her green shirt. She had a guitar strapped around her, strumming so feverishly that a small crowd was starting to form around her.

Then Gabriel noticed the booth she was beside. It was the music club. Gabriel walked over to where she was standing and playing her guitar. He stopped at the edge of the crowd and watched her. Her fingers changed from her melodic placement to an intense dance over the strings. The display was nothing short of impressive, especially for Gabriel, who was not musical in the least. The music was captivating.

Jake walked over to Gabriel. He mirrored his line of sight and noticed who Gabriel was looking at. Both of them watched her play for several more seconds. When she stopped she announced, "If you are interested in joining the music club, please sign up. We are planning on doing some shows at the coffee shop on campus, the Colombiana."

Gabriel was so entranced that he forgot what they were there for. "We should get going," he said. "Orientation will be starting soon."

FILE #3

ORIENTATION

The first part of orientation was being held in the Student Union Building's massive auditorium. All kinds of major events happened there—plays, concerts, anything that might draw a crowd. It was a large room with white walls and wood flooring. Large windows along the left side brought a clean light into the room.

Instantly, they could hear a speech from one of the department heads. A woman with shoulder-length auburn hair stood at the podium. She introduced the new professors. While she rattled off names behind the podium, Gabriel saw Coach V sitting off to the side as if hiding in the corner. His hat was once again pulled down low. Gabriel wondered if he ever took that hat off. His head craned from the left to the right, scanning the crowd.

The boys slid into two empty seats in the last row on the right side. The chairs squeaked loudly as they sat down, ruining any chance of being unnoticed. The speaker was stating some of the history of the school, making some grand statement about the importance of the SIA campus. Jake pretended to doze off, and Gabriel nudged him jokingly. Miming a fake snore, Jake stirred in the chair. Gabriel rolled his eyes at Jake's over-the-top clowning around. He turned to listen. Just then the crowd erupted into a fury of applause. Startled by the sudden and deafening sound of clapping, Jake sat straight up. Both of them missed the message from the speaker but attempted to clap along in unison with the crowd.

Gabriel realized quickly that the speaker had introduce the famous Dr. Drake and another man Gabriel didn't recognize. Drake was a famous scientist who worked on campus. Gabriel remembered him from seeing him on the news. Dr. Drake was much older now, but apparently he was a prodigy in his youth, a genius who worked with one of the first scientists to understand the gifted, Dr. Ferentheil. Drake commanded the respect of everyone.

Recalling his history, Gabriel knew that when Ferentheil had passed away in a lab accident, Dr. Drake had been seen as the continuation of all Ferentheil's research. He was the hope that the gifted needed. Drake knew so much about the gifted. Without him, many believe the gifted would not be where they are today.

The crowd cheered for several more seconds before Dr. Drake made his way to the podium. He stood on a stool to see over the podium as he only stood about five feet at best. His long white hair was brushed back. A clean, white lab coat draped over his body, zipped up to his neck.

Dr. Drake did not speak long. He opened with a few words in his raspy voice on the integrity of the school, how the school was forged from the need for something better.

"Our school, the Sabot Institute, is a beacon of progress, the Eden to which the world looks to for hope. We will push the bounds of what is possible and make a way for perfection. We work with both gifted and nongifted students to make sure the world is progressing onward in safety, harmony, and advancement."

Then Dr. Drake paused. All of a sudden he coughed in his hand as if to stop himself. He looked at his podium and then returned his gaze to the crowd. "Allow me to introduce a man most of you recognize, Marcus James."

Marcus James took the microphone and said, "Many of you know me. I am the president of Pharis International, one of the many associations that helps gifted individuals get into amazing careers where they can use their gifts to change this world. Maybe you are able to harness electricity. Well, you could power an entire city with your gift. Or maybe you want to work at one of the world-renowned agencies helping to protect the world. Whatever your gift, our company wants to remind you to do your best, and one day maybe you could work for us."

With a massive cheer and applause, the crowd erupted at Mr. James's words. He waved and nodded as he backed away from the podium stand and returned to his seat. After several minutes of cheering, the keynote speaker welcomed Coach V forward. He was not one for the spotlight, and Gabriel could tell he was uncomfortable. He stood up, towering over the podium.

The coach was a massive figure, with broad shoulders and thick forearms. His dark skin was offset by his white shirt, and over his head he wore the same hat he wore on the day he recruited Gabriel to the college. His navy-blue hat with the letters *SIA* emboldened on the front. The brow was pulled down tight over his forehead, shadowing his eyes.

Coach broke the tension by admitting his own uneasiness being up front, stage-center. He looked at the crowd, left to right. He paused and coughed into his hand. Then he spoke. "Eighty-seven years ago, this school did not exist. Eighty-seven years ago the first baptism happened. A day where the first people that came to be called the gifted received strange, new abilities they couldn't understand."

The crowd was silent. It was a story they'd all heard, but the command that Coach V had was unshakable. They all watched and listened intently.

"At first these people were outcasts. They were ridiculed. Some humans were afraid of them while others were still hopeful. An American senator named Saul Fairsea was one of the first to propose that gifted be removed from the general public and forced into segregated communities."

The crowd fell eerily silent.

"But then another man—the champion of the gifted, some called him—named Paul Damascus rose as a help to the gifted. He was the man who even coined the term 'gifted' and stated that we could help the humans. That we could bring about prosperity for the whole world. He initiated the Protector Program. He started the GEM, or the Gifted Education Mandate, which created gifted educational departments, so gifted kids could become valuable parts of our workforce. Now all around the world, countries have enacted the same programs to get gifted into their workforce and help their countries and continents."

He paused.

"You are here for one purpose. All of our students, gifted or not, are here to change the world. I hope you all take me serious when I say we all can make the world a better place."

Every head in the crowd was nodding in reply.

"Here you won't be judged by whether you're gifted or not, but by your ability to change the world!" Then Coach V stepped away from the microphone, and the crowd exploded into applause.

With that, the keynote speaker returned and clapped cheerfully. After the cheering died down, he instructed everyone to head to their departments. He explained that if they weren't completed online already, they would do so today.

Against one of the glass walls of the auditorium were several tables with people sitting there. Above the tables were several banners for various accomplishments. Gabriel noticed there were a few for Coach V's sparring team. About half of the crowd of students moved toward the tables, while the rest left to continue signing up for clubs.

Each gift was broken down into various groups, and each group had its own department. Gabriel stood up and looked for the kinetics department. Spotting his department, Gabriel started walking toward the kinetics table. Jake followed him.

Gabriel and Jake looked at each other. Jake had a shocked look on his face. He realized that although he'd showed Gabriel his own gift, Jake hadn't asked Gabriel what his gift was. "I didn't even ask you what your gift was."

"Yeah, my gift is telekinesis. I didn't tell you?" Gabriel stated full of excitement.

Jake laughed. "No, I can't believe we are in the same department!"

The kinetics department was devoted to those who had the ability to manipulate matter of some sort. These were some of the most in-demand gifts because of the power they could produce. Many of the students in the department were able to control various elements, such as water, ice, or in Jake's case, fire.

The line was long, with all the new gifted students who were entering the institute. Gabriel was standing beside Jake, not really in line but just hovering beside it. Gabriel looked over to him and said, "Don't get too far from the line."

"Sorry, I don't like long lines," Jake answered. "I'll stand over here."

Behind Gabriel there was a loud-mouthed student who kept complaining about the slow pace of the line. He started off with loud moans and groans as the line crawled closer. Then he started making comments about the staff and how feeble they must be for the line to move so slowly.

Then he directed his verbal attacks on Gabriel. He must have seen Gabriel's form over his shoulder, because he asked, "Is your first name Galterio?"

"Huh?" Gabriel asked with a horrific expression on his face.

"Your paper, it said Galterio Gabriel Green. Your first name is Galterio?" he asked. "What a weird name."

"Uh," Gabriel said, starting to stutter.

Just then Jake stepped up. "What's your name, String Bean?" asked Jake with a tone matching the unknown boy's tone.

"Bernard," he answered. "Why?"

With a smirk, Jake decided to give him a taste of his own medicine. "Listen, Bernie, my buddy over here is one of the coolest kids on campus. He's a topnotch gifted; he's got more power in his little pinky toe than you do in your whole body. Got it?"

The boy looked from Jake to Gabriel and then back to Jake. Bernie was speechless. So was Gabriel for that matter. Both of them looked at Jake without any idea what to say. Bernard was standing there, holding his mouth agape. Jake sneered at him with an expression that begged him to say something else. Bernard decided to not reply, and he turned and walked away.

Jake looked at Gabriel, his demeanor completely calmed once again. "Man, that guy had some nerve."

"Yeah, wow, thanks, I think," said Gabriel.

"No problem, buddy. You're with me. I have your back," Jake said in reply. After several seconds, he looked back at Gabriel. Then he asked. "What was he going on about with your name?"

Gabriel cringed. He was hoping Jake didn't notice it. Through almost completely clenched teeth, he said, "My first name isn't Gabriel. It's Galterio. But I don't go by Galterio. It's more of a family name. It's tradition. My father is Galterio Angelo and my grandfather is Galterio Marco."

The line took one small step forward. Jake looked at Gabriel. Gabriel could tell what he was thinking.

"So your full name is Galterio Gabriel Green?" Jake asked.

"Yup," Gabriel answered.

"Wow, that is a lot of Gs," Jake stated.

After about ten minutes, Gabriel and Jake were at the front of the line. In front of them were two assistants sitting at a table with a blue-and-silver covering on it. They looked like robots with laptops in front of them, typing away feverishly. Gabe handed the female assistant on the left a form, as did Jake with the assistant on the right.

The woman looked at the paper and began typing again as if the world was about to end if she didn't type a mile a minute. Then she held her hand over a blank piece of paper. Her eyes grew darker, and then Gabriel noticed the paper had text all over it. As she moved her hand over the paper, the text appeared. This was one gift Gabriel hadn't seen before. He had heard that these scribing gifts were very handy in offices, because they could print documents quicker than machines. The female assistant grabbed the printed paper and read it over for any errors.

She then looked up at Gabriel. "ID?" she said in a tone that could be a question or statement.

Frozen for a second, Gabriel realized what she wanted. "Oh, yeah. Here it is." He handed her two small cards for identification, unsure of which one she needed. The first was his state license. Although he didn't own a car, he'd received his license back in high school. The second was his school ID, which he'd received during his summer tour of the campus. It was a poorly taken picture amongst the backdrop of the school's skyline that he'd received in the mail after he'd toured the school.

She looked at it and then at Gabriel. She input a long number and then handed Gabriel a copy of his course schedule with the two ID cards. The course schedule laid out all of his classes for the semester. The first class was kinetics, but beside it the paper had the words *Placement Required.*

"What does 'Placement Required' mean?" asked Gabriel.

"You will need to take a placement exam. You can come to the gymnasium tomorrow morning." Then she handed him another form. It had the times of placement exams.

"Thank you." Then Gabriel added, "I'll go to the first one."

She quickly printed him another form with her hand and signed him up. "Next," she yelled out before Gabriel could even get out of the way.

Gabriel was pushed aside, trying to grab the paper from her. Luckily, he got it and moved as the line forced him off to the side. He looked over it and nodded appreciatively. Jake was on the other side of the line and was doing the same thing. However, Jake was sulking. His eyes bulged out of their sockets, and a grim expression darkened his face. Gabriel walked around the line and met him on the other side.

"What's wrong?" Gabriel asked.

"Have you seen all the classes we have to take?" Jake asked in a tone of terror.

Gabriel laughed. "So, are you going to take your placement test tomorrow?"

"Do I have to?" asked Jake.

"Well, if you want to get placed into a kinetics class, then yes."

"Fine, are you going too?"

Gabriel nodded. "Yes," he stated as well.

***

The following morning, Gabriel awoke bright and early. He looked across the room and saw Jake was still sleeping. Jake was a heavy sleeper. Gabriel arose from his bed and prepared for his morning. Just as he exited the bathroom, Jake was getting up. He didn't look like he wanted to be awake at this hour.

"Hey," Gabriel said in a jovial tone. "Good morning."

Jake sneered and went into the bathroom.

Gabriel made coffee with the small coffee maker they had in their room. It wasn't good coffee, even by college-freshman standards. Jake poured himself a cup after he was dressed. He took a sip without any milk or cream. Gabriel winced when he saw Jake take a sip.

Instantly, Jake recoiled. He shook his head and stuck out his tongue. "What did you make?" he asked.

"It's coffee," Gabriel replied.

"This isn't coffee," Jake exclaimed in disagreement, but Gabriel couldn't help but laugh a little bit.

After sipping one more gulp, Jake went to the door. "Well, let's get this placement exam over with."

The boys found a large group of students outside the gymnasium. Coach V was there with a clipboard and a stack of papers. He was filling out the forms when Gabriel walked up to him. "How are you, Coach V?" he asked.

"Well, if it isn't Gabriel. Gabriel Green. It is good to see you, son. How's the family?"

He extended a meaty fist, and Gabriel shook his hand. Coach V was in a large navy-blue button-up shirt with the school's logo imprinted on the left chest pocket. A thin layer of sweat shimmered in the sunlight over his dark skin. He removed his hat and wiped his forehead with his sleeve.

"Warm out, isn't it?" Jake added.

"Oh, Jake Burns," stated Coach V, not having noticed Jake yet. "My newest recruit."

Jake shook his hand and greeted Coach as well.

"So, you boys are here for the placement exam, aren't you?" asked V.

"Yes, sir," answered Gabriel.

"So, I think you are the last ones I am waiting for," stated Coach V. "Let's go over the procedure."

Coach V blew his whistle to call the class's attention. "All right, folks, let's gather up over here." The group formed around him. All of the students were looking at Coach V as they huddled together.

"We are going to be running some drills. This will allow me to determine if you need to be in Kinetics 101 or Kinetics 201. Some of you may have received basic training or have progressed in your gift enough to not need the basics we cover in 101."

Gabriel's heart instantly began thumping in his chest. He wanted to perform well, but he wasn't sure how he would do. Then he started feeling nervous that his headaches would cripple him again.

"If you are advanced enough, we will place you in 201. But that's if you really show us something impressive. Now just do your best, all right?" Coach V added.

Next, Coach V split them into groups. Gabriel wasn't sure how he broke them up, but Jake was put into a different group. The first group left with Coach V and entered the gymnasium. It was several minutes before they returned, probably more like half an hour. While the next group went, Gabriel and Jake stretched on the field and waited. After the first two groups went, Jake's group went.

Gabriel remained on the field by himself for another half hour before they returned. Gabriel was in the last group called. There were two others in his group—a girl with short hair that was pulled back into a bun and shone a streak of blue in it, and a younger-looking boy with black hair.

Jake and the other students in his group were exiting the gym, all talking about something. As they entered earshot, Gabriel could tell they were talking about their tests. Gabriel took a few steps over toward Jake, but before he could even ask him how it went, Coach V appeared and called the last group.

As Jake walked by, Gabriel looked at him with a look of uncertainty on his face. It was not so much worry as it was a hopeful expectation on what was going to happen. He entered into the gymnasium, but it was much darker than he'd expected. His eyes had a hard time adjusting from the bright summer sun. Gabriel was reminded of his father not lighting up the house when they were in the depths of winter in an attempt to keep the electric bill down. He wondered if the lights weren't on because the semester hadn't officially begun.

They were brought to a large room with a large swimming pool in the center, well-lit with underwater lights. The water reflected light onto the walls with a shimmering pattern as the water softly moved left and right. Coach V coughed in his hand, his usual way of calling for attention.

All three of the students looked over at Coach V standing at the edge of the water. "All right, everyone," he said in his deep voice. "I have a test for each of you, using this water."

Gabriel wondered what exactly he had in mind for them all using the same water. "Zoey, you will be first," Coach V said with a welcoming tone.

Gabriel and the other boy were directed to move to the corner of the room. Zoey was instructed to move the water with her mind. Instantly, Gabriel assumed she was a hydrokinetic, a water user whose gift allowed her to manipulate water molecules by thought. In complete amazement, Gabriel watched. First, she pulled out a glob of water and struggled to maintain the water in a mass.

Amazed and excited, Gabriel couldn't help himself. "Awesome," he whispered to himself, smiling from ear to ear.

Not even noticing Gabriel, Coach had her move the sphere of water in the air as high as she could manage. As it lifted, the water began to lose its shape. Before it reached the ceiling, Zoey lost control of the sphere. She tried to catch it and maintain its circular shape, but it was too late—she'd lost her concentration on the orb.

Coach V scribbled something on the papers he had on his clipboard. Then he turned back to Zoey. "I understand your ability doesn't just allow you to control water."

She nodded, somewhat shyly.

"Can you demonstrate it for me?" Coach V asked, coaxing her out of her shyness.

In answer, she walked to the edge of the pool and stood there. She breathed in deeply. Then she kicked off her black flip-flops. Her left foot stretched down to the cool, blue water, and her toes broke the surface. Immediately, her entire body changed from skin and bones to clear water. However, within a few minutes the young lady had a hard time maintaining her water form. She fell over and splashed into a puddle.

Gabriel's eyes widened. He was terrified, thinking the worst had happened. "Is she—?" he asked.

However, Coach V interrupted him. "It's fine. Ferentheil's laws say that no one can hurt themselves with their own gift."

"So, she's all right?" asked Gabriel.

As if in reply to Gabriel's question, the pool of water started moving. Then the water began to congeal and reform into a solid shape. Quickly, the girl Zoey returned to her form, lying on the ground. She was breathing deeply, her sides rising and falling while she remained on the ground.

Coach V held out his hand and lifted her up. She was still panting and exhaling intensely. Coach V nodded in approval. "That was impressive, Zoey." Then he handed her a towel for her drenched hair and clothes.

She dried off, and Coach V handed her a form with red circles and handwritten notes. Gabriel watched from the opposite side of the pool, but he couldn't hear what the coach said because the pool's filter suddenly kicked on and made a churning sound beneath him. Then Zoey turned and walked out of the pool room.

Coach V called over the next student. His test was not nearly as interesting as Zoey's. Apparently, the young man had the ability to hold his breath under water. So Coach V had him time his ability underwater. Gabriel sat around for several minutes while Coach V had the boy perform some small tasks underwater. It seemed to take forever for the exam to be finished, but it was also an impressive feat. Gabe couldn't help but be impressed.

Finally, it was Gabriel's turn. He was summoned over to Coach V as the other boy walked away with his form. Gabriel wondered how the other boy had done. Gabe hadn't really seen the boy's performance, because Gabe had spaced out here and there.

However, now was his time. A nervous anticipation coursed through Gabriel as he approached Coach V and stood there in front of him. Coach V looked him in the eyes. His deep, dark eyes were the color of obsidian with flecks of orange. Gabe had never seen eyes so dark but still so shiny. Coach coughed in his hand.

"We have two tasks I want you to perform. These will be a pretty good gauge of your power grade."

"My grade?" asked Gabriel.

"Yes," answered Coach. "Your power grade is the level of your gift. Several things go into your grade." Then he paused thinking of the qualifications. "Uh, dexterity, control, durability, and potential."

"We start with D grade, which is usually a weak or newly developed gifted."

Gabriel nodded.

"Then C grade is more developed but still has a low level of ability and application."

"So, they can start to use their ability, but still not very well," Gabriel said, mostly asking.

Coach V nodded. "Exactly. Then we go into B grade and A grade, which are more developed and have good control and sync with their ability."

"So, A grade is the strongest?" Gabriel asked.

"No," Coach stated flatly. "There is another level that few gifted ever reach. But we call a gifted with complete control over their gift and perfect sync an S grade."

"Wow," Gabriel said, leaving his mouth wide open.

Coach V shook his head. "I'm sorry. I was supposed to be examining your ability, not lecturing you on the grading system."

Gabriel smiled and chuckled in reply. "It's all right. It sounds interesting."

Coach V moved to face the water. He held his hand out and said, "Gabriel, I want you to hit the water with all of the force you can muster."

"You mean like punch it?" he asked.

"No, no, no, I want you to push out a powerful force of telekinetic energy and hit the water with it. The nice thing about water is you can smash it as much as you want and not break it. So it is the perfect way to test how much force you are putting out."

Gabriel's head rolled to the right, and he let out a long oh.

So, Gabriel centered himself as Coach V told him to do. He breathed in deeply, letting his lungs fill with the chlorine-scented air. Then he exhaled. With one swift motion of his arms, he threw it out and a telekinetic force hit the pool and splashed the water back. Gabriel sighed. He wasn't very pleased with himself.

Coach V coughed in his hand, and Gabriel looked over at him. Coach said, "Gabriel, you need to release your mind. I think you restraining yourself. Now with your imagination, visualize yourself pushing the water with all your might."

This time Gabriel really focused. He imagined himself throwing all of the water out of the pool with his mind. He saw a large wave crashing over the side of the pool. Then he threw out an arm in a punching motion. The kinetic energy threw the water up into a colossal wave that spilled over the side of the pool and washed over the wall.

When Gabriel opened his eyes, the whole far side of the pool room was dripping wet from the tidal wave that Gabriel created. His mouth gaped, astonished at what he had done.

Coach V had an impressed look over his face. "Well, I think your potential is as high as I expected," he exclaimed with a laugh in his voice. "Now to see how your dexterity and control are."

He had Gabriel try and part the water of the pool on two sides. Gabriel found it was nearly impossible to move the swishing liquid. It was like trying to hold, well, water. It kept pouring over and spilling into the center. When he got one side under control, the other side began to pour and slosh and spill.

Meanwhile, Coach V scribbled something on his clipboard. While Gabriel was still trying to hold the water back, Coach V finished writing and hollered to Gabriel that he was done. Gabriel removed his telekinetic barriers, and the water rushed back into the center of the pool with a mighty splash, causing the water to shoot up in the air.

Gabriel dropped to a knee. His head was throbbing again, a massive tension headache that stretched from the back of his head down into his neck. He gripped his neck and massaged it forcefully, trying to stop the pain that felt like daggers stabbing his neck, sending massive, agonizing bolts through his body.

Coach V knelt beside Gabriel. "Here, put your hand here," he told Gabriel. Then Coach showed him where to put his hands, pointing to his temples and telling him to massage there.

"Do you frequently get headaches when you use your power?" asked Coach.

"No," Gabriel answered through a groan. "Only if I overdo it."

After a few minutes of massaging his temples, Gabriel felt better.

Coach V then said, "You should drink plenty of fluids. Your gift is extremely potent and uses up a good amount of your body's energy. Staying hydrated will help you to not feel the effects of it quite as much."

"Thanks," Gabriel said, standing back up. "What class should I be in?"

"I think you have a lot of potential, Gabriel, and you have the makings of one of the strongest gifted I have ever seen."

"Thank you," Gabriel replied.

"I thought about putting you in the more advanced Kinetics 201. However, I feel you would benefit from the essential training you will get in my Kinetics 101 course," Coach finished, handing Gabriel a form with the typed words *Kinetics 101* circled in red ink.

FILE #4

LOST

The weekend arrived before Gabriel realized it. The week was so hectic that the weekend was a welcome change of pace. He had been assigned his classes and shopped for some last-minute essentials. He and Jake wandered the campus to familiarize themselves with the place. By Saturday afternoon, he felt that he was ready for Monday and the start of classes.

Gabriel also saw his first sparring match on Saturday. It wasn't an official sparring match, seeing as how the season didn't start until the spring. However, Coach V organized a friendly match against another school's team. Gabriel sat in the stands while Jake was on the bench. Unfortunately, Gabriel wasn't familiar with the rules or the competition. However, it seemed to be similar to wrestling or fencing.

Points were awarded for downing your opponent. Unlike in those sports, this allowed the use of gifts in the ring, but competitors weren't allowed to use their powers without restraint. A referee was in the metal holding cell that surrounded the ring to make sure that no fighter hurt the other without penalty.

Jake didn't compete in any matches. Being so new to the team, Coach V didn't start him. He wasn't even a substitute.

That evening, the boys prepared for their soccer game. Gabriel got ready and headed down to the Quad, where Jake was supposed to meet him after he went for a run. They didn't talk much after Jake's match, but Gabriel got the impression that Jake was upset he didn't get to compete. Maybe that's why he needed to go on a run.

Down on the Quad, Gabriel spotted Jake standing by a vending machine. He was breathing heavily from his run, bracing himself against the vending machine. As Gabriel got closer, Jake turned toward Gabriel and held out his sweaty hand to greet Gabriel. The moment they connected hands, Gabriel shot back in fright. Gabriel looked at his hand, and it was a bright shade of pink. He looked up at Jake with concern in his eyes.

Jake's eyes were wide and full of remorse. Gabriel looked from Jake to the hand that Gabe was waving to shake off the pain.

"I'm sorry. I'm sorry. Burn it all," Jake said as a curse.

Gabriel smirked at the expression, which was popular one these days. But it was funny hearing Jake using it. "It's all right," he answered, still shaking his hand. "It just caught me off guard."

"It's a side effect of my gift. It happens when I work out a lot. I usually take an ice-cold shower after practice to help cool down," Jake answered with a hopeful laugh. "But since we are playing soccer tonight, I figured why bother with a shower."

With Gabriel's hand no longer feeling like it was a melted marshmallow, the boys left for the gymnasium. Halfway down the Quad, Jake apologized again. Gabe brushed it off like it was no big deal, although his hand did feel unusually stiff. "It's all right. It wasn't as bad as it could have been. Just scared me really."

Trying to play it cool, Gabriel smirked at Jake to let him know it as all going to be all right. The burn was not severe enough to scar or cause any damage. However, the sheer intensity of the heat was enough to cause Gabriel to wonder how it was even possible to control.

There wasn't much time to ponder Jake's gift, because they were just about to the gymnasium. It was built like a typical school building, with the same pale stone bricks and glass. Despite its simplicity, the massive structure had a certain grandness to it, reminding Gabriel of the Roman Coliseum.

As he walked past, Gabriel noticed an etching carved into the wall beside the entrance. It was a phrase. Gabriel had to step back to catch the whole thing. As he stood there, he read, *Humility is the first step toward greatness.* Gabriel smiled as he read the inscription on the wall. He must have not noticed it earlier because of the crowds going into the sparring match, but he thought that was a fitting phrase.

Jake stood at the door, looking at Gabriel. Realizing that he had been standing there for several seconds, staring at the engraving in the wall, Gabriel snapped to with a shake of his head. He then walked to the door behind Jake. The opening of the gym was a small room with a desk. To the left and right were hallways and in front of them were two sets of double doors that led into the main arena.

Once inside the arena, Jake showed him where he usually worked out. Although he had only been on the team for a week, Jake walked around the place like a seasoned veteran. He played up how important certain exercise machines were and showed off some of the integral parts of the gymnasium for workout routines.

Then Gabriel noticed a whooshing sound and looked behind himself. He saw two figures sparring in the ring across the massive room. He couldn't make out any distinguishing features because of the distance and the fact that the room wasn't fully lit, but the two were throwing jabs and kicks with an extreme intensity. The fighters seemed so focused that Gabriel could barely believe it. Just then, one of them released a massive surge of electricity from his hands. It smashed into the large metal cage that enclosed the ring and then disappeared.

"Wow!" exclaimed Gabe.

Jake chuckled. "Yeah. That's Lucien; they call him the 'Meister.' His gift is the ability to control electricity."

Gabe was speechless. His mouth was gaping as he watched.

"Hmm," Jake said, looking at the scene. "The other must be Jin. She's superfast and agile. I don't really know her power. She is just amazing, though."

Slowly, the rest of the students came in for the indoor soccer game. They met on the track that went around the rest of the arena, and they began to stretch. Gabriel couldn't help but be distracted by the spectacle going on in the ring behind them. During the stretching, Gabriel repeatedly found himself gazing over at their sparring match.

Soon, the whole group for the soccer game seemed to be present. So they headed to the indoor soccer arena next door. It was a moderately large room with curved edges instead of corners. The high, white walls almost made it hard to perceive depth, but luckily there was a stripe that ran down the sides that helped.

The head of the sports club came to the middle of the turf and high-fived Jake, and then they did an elaborate handshake where they connected hands, then elbows, and shook their arms back and forth.

When he left, Gabe asked Jake, "Who is that?"

"That's Eames. He's on the sparring team too. You probably saw him compete today."

Eames called for everyone's attention, but only the closest looked at him. So he rushed around the entire group at superhuman speeds. Everyone's attention was immediately on the whirling figure running around them. At that moment, Eames returned to the center before anyone could even see.

With everyone's mouths wide open, Eames stated, "Thank you! Now let's play some soccer."

The students were broken up into two teams. Eames called an athletic girl up to be the opposing captain with him, and they began calling out students for their teams. Jake ended up on one team and Gabriel on another. Then they handed out different-colored shirts, headbands, and arm bands for the two sides. Gabriel's team wore yellow pennies, and Jake's team was in red. Each side had eleven on their team including the two boys.

From across the pitch, Gabe and Jake glared at each other intensely. Both knew they were going to win, and both were determined to show the other what kind of athlete he was today—Gabriel, the footballer, and Jake, the perpetual wrestler. Although they were from different sport backgrounds, each of them possessed a certain basic athleticism that translated to all sports. Each was quick, strong, and agile: the basic qualities of a good athlete.

Eames called for everyone to listen. "All right, everyone. All gifts are a go. Use whatever upper hand you have, but make sure you keep it safe. Anyone gets hurt and the club could get shut down. So be careful and watch out for each other."

Just then Coach V walked into the room. Instantly every eye in the room locked onto him. No one dared speak before the daunting figure as Coach V stood in silence for a few seconds. Gabriel remembered the day he met the coach. Gabriel thought Coach V was the kind of person he wanted to be like— respected not because of things he did, but because of the kind of man he was.

Gabriel realized that Coach V was monitoring the game. He blew the whistle, and Gabriel's team kicked the ball to their center-middle player, Eames. The other team rushed at Eames, but no normal speed could compare to Eames's gift. Instantly, Gabriel realized what speed really was. Although Eames was able to outpace all of the players, he couldn't keep control of the ball no matter how hard he tried. Within a few seconds, Eames tripped over the ball and fell to the turf with a thud.

Fortunately, Gabriel was right behind him for support. He trapped the ball with his right foot. Scanning the field, he looked for anyone in yellow. Down the left side, he saw a tall girl sprinting down the field quickly. She threw up her hand as she neared the goal. Aiming as best he could, Gabriel chipped the ball and sent it over the defense. It dropped down just in front of the attacker, and she delivered a terrific kick to put it in the back of the net for a goal.

Everyone screamed ecstatically, no one more so than the girl who'd scored. She ran up and hugged Gabriel, catching him off guard. His face turned as red as Jake's shirt. She wrapped her arms around his neck and cheered his fantastic pass. Gabriel tried to hide his awkward smile as everyone congratulated him.

The team surrounded him, patting him on the back and yelling, "Excellent placement!" and "Perfect put!" and "Great chip!"

Then one of the other players complained. "That was cheap. He used his gift. I'm not impressed. Anyone with telekinesis could do that."

Of course, Gabriel thought. It was Bernard.

Eames walked past Bernie on his way to his side of the field. "Don't be dense, Bernard. It's super ball. Of course we are going to use our gifts. Okay?"

"Whatever," Bernard said in a mocking tone.

Gabriel smiled again and returned to his side of the pitch.

Eames collected his team back on their side. The other team started with the ball. After a minute of pressure on Gabe's team, Jake's team kept the ball on their side of the field. Then Jake found the ball on the center of the field. He was surrounded by yellow shirts. He decided to use his physical force, and he powered through two defenders. Eames rushed from the other side and got in front of Jake. At the eighteen-yard line, Jake ripped a powerful shot. Eames jumped to intercept, but he was just out of reach as the ball sailed over his head.

The goalie used his gift of body growth, stretching out to catch the ball. However, the force of the ball caught him by surprise, and he fell back into the goal with the ball in his hand.

Jake pumped his arm as his team cheered around him. Gabriel came up behind him and said, "Great shot, man. But I wouldn't expect anything less from the world's strongest fire man!"

Jake laughed. He answered back, "That's the worst nickname ever!"

Gabriel laughed and dropped his head saying, "Yeah, I know. Sorry about that."

The game continued. The score went back and forth for several minutes. First, Gabriel scored on a perfect pass that he tapped in the far corner, and then Jake assisted in a pass that ended in the goal. The teams were pretty evenly matched.

Gabriel couldn't help but think that if Eames could control the ball better, he could be unstoppable. But the ball just wouldn't keep up with his tremendous speed. If he could keep the ball at his speed, no one could catch him. Or maybe he could slow down enough to dribble the ball.

The clock dwindled down to just a matter of moments left. With less than two minutes left, Jake's team was moving down the field with the ball. Bernard eluded down the left side of the field. Jake was sprinting down the opposite side. Pushing past the defenders all around him. Jake got in front of the goal, and Bernard kicked up a pass to Jake. Instinct took over, and Jake jumped in the air, throwing his right leg up over his head to make contact with the ball.

He kicked, and the ball rocketed off the top crossbar and bounced into the goal. The powerful shot caused something in the metal beam that made up the post for the goal to come loose. Jake crashed on the ground, head and shoulders first, landing with a painful crack. Jake sat there hurt and stunned for a moment. He was unaware that the goalpost was coming loose.

As he remained motionless on the ground, the goalpost swayed back and forth. Jake's shot had been so forceful that it unhinged it. The motion caught Jake's attention. He looked up. The metal beam started to drop toward him.

Jake's survival instincts took hold, and he threw up an arm to block the falling metal. Several seconds passed. No pain. No smashing pressure coming down on him. There should have been a pain, agony, or something.

Realizing he was shaking, Jake opened his left eye. Looking up, he noticed the metal beam. Instinctively, he closed his eye again. When he looked back up, it wasn't falling. It was just hovering there. By now the rest of the players were around him. A few helped him get to his feet. Two others moved the beam back into position.

Eames and three others locked the whole goalie stand into place as Jake watched them. Eames and the others said that the beam hadn't been locked into place before the match. Whoever used the field last must have not put it into place correctly.

Unable to stand, Jake knelt on the ground, holding his back and shoulder.

"That was you, wasn't it?" Jake asked, looking up at Gabriel. Gabriel realized that Jake knew it had been Gabriel who'd caught it with his gift and kept it from falling down on him.

"Don't worry about it, man. We are roommates. Right?" he stated. "You got my back, and I got yours."

Jake looked up at his friend. Could this be what it was like to have a friend? Was this the feeling of loyalty being acted out in a real way. Unknown to Gabriel, but Jake had never had a friend like this.

"It looks like you scored the winning goal. Game over. Nice job," Gabriel said, kneeling.

He then helped Jake up and helped him to the sidelines. There they got him some ointment for Jake's upper back, which appeared to be bruised quite fiercely.

"He might have a concussion. You can't let him get to sleep," stated Eames. "Let's bring him to the medical room in the gymnasium."

So Gabriel and Eames escorted the injured Jake to the medical room. Together they helped him get onto a gurney. The nurse was a soft-voiced, middle-aged woman with a poufy, curly hairdo. She checked Jake for any signs of a concussion.

"I don't think you have one, but why don't we keep you here overnight just to be sure."

She then looked at Jake's back. It seemed to be bruising, so she gave him some ice to help keep it from swelling. Gabriel walked over to her while she was applying the cold compress.

"Ma'am, am I allowed to stay with him?" he asked.

"I'm sorry. We generally don't allow friends to stay this late. You can come visit him in the morning. He should be fine here until then," she said in a soft but firm tone of voice.

The following morning, Gabriel woke up early to visit Jake. He was worried about how he was feeling and wanted to make sure he wasn't still hurt. So Gabriel quickly readied himself and left his dorm room. He locked the door and sped down the stairs of the building. Then he rounded the corner and moved through the metal double doors.

Outside it was a cool, crisp morning. The ground was lightly covered in a layer of mist that would probably be gone within the hour. The summer sun was just breaking over the trees that surrounded the campus, and it warmed the air. Fall was quickly approaching, and Gabriel could feel it in the air.

Before too long, Gabriel was at the gymnasium. Jake would probably still be asleep, but Gabriel was too anxious to wait until later. He pushed through the large gymnasium doors and entered the lobby of the gym, turning to head down the hallway. It took him a few minutes to find the medical room, because yesterday he had been coming from the opposite direction. Finally, he found the room after some looking.

When he came to the window and saw the words Medical Facility on the door, he peered inside but couldn't see Jake. He knocked on the door, but no one answered. He stood at the door for almost ten minutes before anyone came by. Then a voice came from just down the hall.

"Hello," a male voice said in an almost questioning tone. "Can I help you?" the voice asked as it came closer.

Immediately Gabriel turned to the voice. He saw a young man, probably another student. "Hey, I'm Gabriel Green. I'm just checking on my friend Jake Burns."

"Oh, hey, yeah, I'm the intern at the medical facility. Mrs. Jay asked me to come open up this morning. She told me there was a young man sleeping off an injury from last night. I'll let you in."

The young man pulled out his keys and unlocked the door, entering first, followed immediately by Gabriel. Panic struck Gabriel. He looked from left to right. He rounded the door to get a better view but saw nothing. The room was completely empty.

His head turned to the young intern. "Where is he?"

"I don't know," the man answered. "Let me check the log. Maybe Mrs. Jay discharged him."

Then the intern grabbed the clipboard on the edge of the bed that Jake had been in last night. He flipped through the attached pages, his expression growing more and more puzzled with each page he turned.

With an air of extreme bewilderment, the boy looked up and said, "No, he wasn't released from the medical room."

"So where is he?" demanded Gabriel, much more forcefully than last time.

"I don't know. The door was locked from the inside. Maybe he just left."

Gabriel wasn't happy with that answer, but he realized that was a possibility, knowing Jake's personality. Instantly, his head dropped, and he said, "Maybe you're right.

"Sorry I couldn't be more help."

Gabriel left the gymnasium and search for Jake. He went to the café called the Colombiana, but there was no Jake. Then at lunchtime he went to the pizzeria on campus, but there was still no sign of Jake. After checking out the dorm room, gym, and Quad, Gabriel was completely out of ideas on where he could be.

As the sun set in the sky, Gabriel realized he'd spent his entire last day of summer without doing anything fun. The fall semester began tomorrow, and still there was no sign of Jake. It was as if he had disappeared without a trace. So, with a slow, depressed gait, he walked to the cafeteria that was attached to the Student Union Building through a tunnel. The cafeteria was a large open room with wood-paneled walls. A retro neon sign read Open over the counter.

Gabriel slid through the line and ordered a sandwich and a soda. Afterward he returned to his dorm room and finished his sandwich. Without much effort, Gabriel dozed off.

THE FIRST DAY

That morning, Gabriel woke up early and went to class. He stood nervously outside the door, knowing that this was the start of the rest of his life. He knew the importance of a good beginning, wanting to make a good impression on his classmates, professors, and friends. He looked over his shoulder, hoping to see Jake. He wasn't sure where he was, but he was hoping he would make it to class.

With one last big, deep breath he walked into the classroom where several students sat in seats in the room. A small group stood to the side talking. Most of the students seemed to have the same nervousness Gabriel had in his eyes—not wanting to make fools of themselves at a new school.

The class was called Power Under Control, and it was required of all of the freshmen students, because it was a foundational class on the importance of using gifts for the improvement of mankind. Above most other classes, this was one of the most important classes.

Quickly, Gabriel walked down the center-aisle steps of the auditorium classroom to find a seat. He was reminded of a movie theater, where the back seats were higher than the front, only this theater people entered from the top. Gabriel noticed what must have been a professor walking in the back door down on the floor. He was an older man, with all-white hair, styled up.

The professor put his brown leather briefcase on the small desk and turned to the podium eyeing the class as Gabriel swung into a seat. Gabriel looked up and saw a blond boy sitting across the aisle. It was Jake.

Just then the professor spoke with a booming voice.

"Hello, I'm Dr. Einrich," said the professor. "I'm the dean of the university."

Gabriel's eyes widened.

The professor continued, "Yes, I'm *that* dean. I'm in charge of the university. I teach only this one course, and the reason I teach this course is because it's the most important."

Gabriel was shocked. He hadn't realized that the class was taught by the most powerful man on campus.

"This class is the most important class you will take on campus not because of what you will learn from me but because of what you will learn from yourself," the professor added.

He paused for several seconds allowing the weight of what he'd said to sink into the class.

"Before we delve too deep into the text, I want you to group up with the people around you and discuss something. I want you to ask yourselves why you are here."

Gabriel looked to the students on his left and then his right. The girl in front of him turned around, and he recognized her immediately—the girl from the other day, the musician who'd played before orientation. She asked Gabriel and the students sitting beside him if they wanted to group up.

The small group went around in a circle and talked about their reasons for wanting to come to the school. There was no law that made the gifted students come to the Sabot Institute of America. However, many students came because it really the best way to figure out what their gifts really were and how to use them.

Then the red-haired girl went next, stating her name was Serena. She paused for a second after giving her name. "Well, I guess I'm here to figure out my power like everyone else." There was another long pause. "But I really want to work on my music too," she added. "I think that's it."

Two more people went. When the turn came to Gabriel, he stated, "Hey, I'm Gabriel Green. I grew up in Bethlehem, not too far from here. I was the only kid in my town that was gifted. The reason I'm here is that when my sister was born, she almost didn't make it. Thankfully the doctors did everything they could and saved her."

The whole group let out a sigh of relief when Gabriel said his sister was all right.

"So from that day on, I wanted to help people. When I was baptized with these gifts, I realized I was given a chance to help people. Then I met Coach V, and he recruited me to the school. He challenged me to come to the school and make this world a better place."

Everyone nodded and Serena clapped her hands softly in a golf clap. Just then Dean Einrich called the class back to attention. He passed out a stack of papers and asked everyone to take one. Gabriel grabbed a form and then passed the stack on to the next person. Looking at the top of the paper, Gabriel saw that it read, "Power Under Control Syllabus." Thumbing through the stack of stapled-together papers, Gabriel read that it explained the class. The second page had due dates for assignments and required books for reading.

"So this is the syllabus, if you have any questions refer to this for all due dates, required materials, or anything else."

Gabriel continued skimming over the form. He saw the books he'd need to look up and all the papers he'd have to write. It seemed like a huge amount of work, so Gabe braced himself to take it all on this semester.

After he'd explained the coursework for the semester, answered some questions, and thoroughly explained his expectations, Dean Einrich dismissed the class and wished them a good day.

Gabriel rushed over to Jake. As they walked out of the classroom together, Gabriel asked Jake where he'd been yesterday.

"All I remember is waking up this morning from my bed. I guess one of the nurses helped me get back to my room, because I honestly don't even remember waking up."

Gabriel was somewhat shocked that Jake didn't remember his entire day. However, he couldn't pursue the topic too much longer because they were about to head into their next class together. They entered their history class, which looked very similar to their last classroom.

They entered the room and walked down to a few empty seats. Jake and Gabriel sat next to each other. Just then Serena sat down next to Gabriel. She smirked at him.

"Hey, we have the same schedule, huh?" she said smiling.

"Yeah, it would seem so. I have science after lunch. Are you in that class?" asked Gabriel.

She nodded. "I have science with Dr. McManus."

Gabriel smirked. "Us too."

Suddenly Gabriel felt less nervous than he had been that morning. Sitting between Jake and Serena, Gabriel felt like maybe he'd found friends. But just as soon as the calm came, a rush of anxiety came over him when the next professor walked into the room. She was a tall, thin woman with a short haircut and black-rimmed glasses who looked as strict as she did smart.

Before anyone could say a word, she was at the front of the room and writing her name on the board. She turned and stared at the class with piercing eyes. Gabriel's stomach lurched as her leering eyes scanned the room.

"I'm Professor White, and this is History of the Gifted. In this class we will chronicle the timeline from the first baptism to now. We will discuss the implications of the gifted in our world and the impacts there of. Also, you will be writing several papers for this class."

The entire class was shell-shocked. Immediately, Gabriel felt that rush of anxiety from the morning, certain he would make a fool of himself in front of this teacher, who seemed to be the type of no-nonsense teacher that stressed him.

"Each paper will be a short, one-page discussion on the themes we discuss in class. You will be required to do extra reading to support the position you will be taking."

Jake looked at Gabriel with dread. Gabriel looked back with a similar expression. Glancing over to Serena, Gabriel noticed that she didn't seem nearly as terrified.

The rest of class was spent going over the syllabus as in the previous class. They discussed some of the topics they would hit over the next semester and some books that would be useful for reading. Professor White dismissed the class not a second early. She didn't seem to be the type to waste a second of class time.

The boys went to lunch, and Serena joined them. They talked more about where they'd come from and what they wanted to gain from SIA. Gabriel told them more about his family, how his father was a cop he wanted to be just like.

Jake interrupted, saying, "I don't think I want to follow my dad's line of work. He was a hotel inspector, so we traveled all over the country, staying in hotels. I was only in schools for a few months at a time, but then we moved, and I had to start all over again."

Gabriel nodded in a gesture of understanding.

"That's probably why I never really liked school too much," Jake stated finally.

"That must have been rough," Serena added.

"It was fine outside of school. We stayed in some really cool places—Palm Beach, New York City, and even California's Venice Beach. That was where we were before I came to SIA. We were there for a long time because there were three hotels my dad had to inspect. So we were there for almost the whole school year."

Serena smirked. "Well that's good."

Jake smiled and said, "Oh yeah, I got into surfing and was able to actually join the wrestling team at that school, because I was there long enough to try out and make the team."

Gabriel smiled at seeing his friend so happy. Then he looked at Serena. "Where are you from?" Gabriel asked.

"Well, I was a foster child. So, I lived in a few places."

Gabriel was somewhat shocked, not sure what to say.

Serena quickly continued. "It's no big deal. I had a few foster families, but I was raised mostly by this one guy. He isn't my biological dad, but he is pretty much my father."

"That's awesome," said Jake. "At least you had someone to take care of you."

She smiled half-heartedly.

After lunch Jake went off to his physical education class while Gabriel and Serena went to their class. The walk was a short one, as the cafeteria was just across the Quad from the Lecture Hall. The Lecture Hall was a large stone building that held many of the large science classes. When they walked in, Gabriel held the door open for Serena.

Serena sat in the second row, but the classroom was so full that there were nowhere to sit for Gabriel. He ended up sitting a few rows behind Serena. Almost as soon as Gabriel sat down, the professor came down the stairs to the podium and placed his briefcase on the desk beside it. An older gentleman with a thin mustache, he wore thick glasses that made his eyes look enormous behind his spectacles.

With a deep Scottish accent that Gabriel recognized immediately, he introduced himself as Professor McManus, his deep voice carrying throughout the room, impressive considering the room was almost twice as large as Gabriel's previous classroom. Then the professor pulled a stack of papers from his briefcase. Similar to the previous classes, he passed them out to the students on the end of the rows and had them pass them onward.

"Here are your course guidelines for this class. I would like to welcome everyone to Science 199, better known as the Study of Venus."

Just then a student stood up from her seat and rushed to the door. She covered her face as she ducked out of the room. The professor smiled and shook his head.

"There is always that one student who is in the wrong room," he said softly. Then he turned back to the class. "Anyway, my name is Dr. McManus. I'm head of the science department here on campus. Please turn to the second page of the papers I passed out."

The class did so, and McManus looked around to see everyone was following along. Then he said, "Right, let's crack on then."

He read several parts of the syllabus to the students and discussed the requirements of the class, which essentially was a study of the source of their gifts. In the not-too-distant past, scientists such as Dr. Drake had learned that the phases and movements of Venus aligned with the baptisms of the gifted.

Then he asked, "Who can tell me what the transit was?"

Several hands rose. He looked from left to right, and his eyes fell on Serena. "Yes, you there."

She answered saying, "The transit refers to the Transit of Venus, when people started developing abilities that we call gifts."

"Yes," Professor McManus said with a long pause. "However, there is so much more there."

He looked around the room at the class. "You would be surprised how many gifted actually don't understand where their gifts, their abilities, come from." He paused again, still looking around the room. "A gifted's unique abilities comes from the gamma radiation from the sun that is altered by the unique atmosphere of the planet Venus."

They spent the remainder of the class time discussing all of the different ideas that McManus had. He explained that Venus was called the "morning star" because it was visible in the morning during sunrise. After some more facts on the planet, he gave some of the details that were more interesting, including the fact that Venus had the longest rotation of any planet in the solar system and that it rotated backward. Many speculated that these factors impacted the gifted.

After class, Gabriel felt as if he'd learned more about Venus than he had about any other planet. He wasn't sure what else he was expected to learn about Venus. He and Serena separated. Gabriel went on to his dorm room while Serena left to meet with her music club.

FILE #6

SIMON SAYS

That evening, Gabriel needed to run to the library to check out some of the books that his professors had mentioned. However, he and Jake were supposed to grab dinner together, so Gabriel waited until Jake got back from practice from the sparring team.

Once Jake returned from practice, he cleaned up and went with Gabriel to the library. Inside, Gabriel told Jake the two books that he needed. Jake went off in one direction, and Gabriel walked down the first row of bookshelves.

"It's not in the history section, dude!" Jake yelled several minutes later.

Jake received several dirty looks, a few coughs, and multiple shushes. However, he just shrugged it off and kept on looking for the books Gabriel had mentioned.

"Any luck?" Jake asked, this time in a quieter register.

"No, it doesn't seem to be here either."

Jake jokingly shivered, feigning sickness, and said, "Well, let's get out of here, man. I can't believe I'm spending my evening in a library to begin with. Let's go to Big Chicago's and grab a slice of pizza!"

Gabriel, who was kneeling down to reach a lower shelf, stood up and punched his palm. "Man, I can't believe it isn't here. My professor said that it would be a really good resource this semester."

"Who burning cares?" Jake replied unsympathetically. "We could be having pizza."

The two boys rounded the corner, and Gabe ran straight into a short young man carrying a huge stack of books in his hands. The teetering stack of books blocked his face and obscured his vision. Gabriel stumbled backward, but caught himself. The other person was sent careening to the ground, books scattering everywhere.

"Oh, man, I'm so sorry!" Gabriel pleaded. He held his hand out to help out the young man. "I'm Gabriel. What's your name?"

"I'm Simon Cruz," the young man added as if he was on an interview.

"Simon Cruz. Nice to meet you," Gabriel stated. "Wait, I've heard about you. Aren't you Dr. Drake's assistant? You're a technopath."

The curly-haired young man looked young, but he was surely no older than twelve. "Not exactly," Simon answered. "I'm an intern in the science department. So, I work in the labs, but not with Dr. Drake directly," Simon answered. There was a pause. Then he added, "I am a technopath though."

Gabriel's mouth dropped. "Wow, that's impressive. How old are you?" he asked.

Looking somewhat embarrassed, Simon answered, "I'm sixteen, but I'm pretty short for my age."

Jake, not one to be impressed by intelligence, rolled his eyes. "So why do you have so many books there, Brainiac?"

Simon picked up a book and brushed it off. Looking at it, he answered, "Oh, these are some books I've wanted to read. So, I figured I'd do that this weekend?"

"You were going to read all of these this weekend?" asked Jake confused.

"Yes, it's just a few science texts on the theoretical progression of abilities, really not too difficult."

"You don't happen to have Gilroy's *Powers to Be*, do you?" Gabe asked.

Simon looked around. "I believe I do." Then it caught his eye, hiding beneath one of his other texts. "Here it is," he said, picking it up.

Handing it to Gabriel, Simon continued, "You can borrow it. I should be fine with just these."

Jake muttered something about Simon's definition of "just" while Simon spoke again.

"No worries," Simon stated.

"Thanks," answered Gabriel, standing up with a stack of books in his hands. "Let me help you get those to the front desk."

Simon thanked Gabe. Gabriel told him it was the least he could do after almost tackling him earlier.

The three boys made their way up the flight of stairs to the main level of the library. Upon reaching the front desk area, they could see the main librarian at his desk, an older gentleman with a thin beard around his jawline. He looked at the boys with their large stacks of books somewhat confused.

"Goodness," he said, "do they have you boys reading all of this already?" He straightened his glasses to make sure he was seeing this all correctly.

Abruptly and quickly, Jake answered back. "No way, this is all his." He pointed at Simon.

"All yours!" the librarian gasped. "But you aren't even a student anymore, Simon."

"Yes, but I'm very interested in these books. I'm just doing some research on gifts."

Once everyone had the books he needed, the boys headed down the Quad and past the Student Union Building. Simon, still being helped by Gabe and Jake, thanked the boys and then asked to know more about them.

As he placed his stack of books on a bench, Gabriel explained who he was, where he was from, that he was a telekinetic, and that this was his first year

"What grade are you?" asked Simon, also taking a break from his books.

"Coach V evaluated us the other day. I'm Grade B," answered Gabriel.

"Really?" answered Simon in return, a tone of intrigue in his voice. "And what about you, Jake?"

"Coach V said he thinks I could be a Grade B. However, my issue causes me some problems. So, until I get that figured out I'm a Grade C pyrokinetic."

Simon's eyes widened. "Ah, such a fascinating ability. What is your 'problem'?" asked Simon, using his fingers to mime air quotes.

Jake recoiled, looking the other way. "Uh, well, I still can't generate flames yet."

"But he sure can heat up his body to extreme temperatures," added Gabriel. "He nearly burned my hand off the other day."

"So, you cannot generate flames by igniting the oxygen molecules in the air. But you have an innate ability to produce extreme heat from your body. Well that's interesting."

Then Simon paused.

"I find all the gifted so interesting. We are like different parts of the body. Some are like hands and others like the feet. We all have tremendous potential and ability, but different functions. Even in the same ability, there are people who express their gifts in different ways. Take you for example, Jake."

Jake looked back at Simon, suddenly drawn into the wording of Simon.

"If all pyrokinesis were a hand. You would be one finger and other pyros would be other fingers. You have the same ability in essence, but it's expressed in a different way. We are all so unique."

Jake turned his head for a moment, trying to comprehend all of what Simon was saying. "I guess I never thought of it that way."

Still gushing, Simon added, "Oh yes, the gifted are truly amazing beings. We have such vast potential. I pray we can fully exploit it and help the world."

Gabriel smiled and nodded in agreement.

Then Simon thought of something. "I'm doing some research on the development in gifts, such as yours. Maybe I could help you."

Gabriel was about to say that they didn't want to take up his time, but Jake immediately said, "That sounds awesome. What can you do?"

***

The boys quickly arrived at a large dormitory, a much larger building than the one that Gabriel and Jake lived in. The building in which they lived was for early students, generally the freshman and sophomores. This was a much nicer building and, according to Simon, used for juniors and seniors.

"I was given special permission to stay here because I'm currently interning at the science lab, and our research is really important to the school. So the school offered me on-campus living." Simon paused for a second. There was an awkward silence as they entered. Then he added, "You remember that kid who was signed to the arena? He lives in this dorm."

Inside, the accommodations were even nicer. The flooring was real hardwood, and the stair railings were beautiful metal fixtures. The doors were a red-stained wood with a glossy finish. They entered Simon's room, and the space alone was almost twice as large as Jake and Gabriel's room. His walls were covered in posters of cartoon characters and scientific puns. One poster was a diagram of the solar system showing the gamma rays that are emitted from the sun and then passed to the planet Venus.

Meanwhile, Simon went directly for his desk, where he slammed the stack of books on the small desk and allowed Gabe and Jake to do the same. Each of them did so, and then Simon sat at the desk. He typed away at the keypad and then looked back to the boys.

"All right, I just ran a quick simulation on this program," Simon stated, pointing to his screen. "If I'm not mistaken, we should be able to replicate the process using your body as the catalyst."

Jake paused him, "The cata-what now?"

"A catalyst, something that causes an accelerated reaction," explained Simon. "So what we can do is have you super heat a part of your body, say your hand, and then that should just need one more thing."

Simon paused for a moment. His eyes space off, looking to the ground but not at the ground, his gaze blank, but his mind entranced. Gabriel could tell he was deep in thought, unaware of anything happening in the physical world.

"Friction!" yelled Simon. "We need friction."

Gabriel snapped his fingers, "Like a match!"

"Do that again," said Simon.

"Do what?"

"That snapping," he repeated. "That's it."

Simon stood up. He began "If we can get your body to get hot enough and then cause just a little bit of friction with a snap. Then you may be able to generate a flame."

Jake looked at Simon with some disbelief, unsure this sort of thing would even work. He looked down at the ground. Then he felt a pressure on his shoulder. He looked to his right and saw Gabriel's hand.

"Hey, what do you have to lose?" asked Gabriel.

"All right," Jake replied. "Let's give it a try."

The boys spent the rest of the day working out the plan to work with Jake on creating this new way of using his power. It seemed farfetched, but Simon convinced Jake. And if it worked, Jake would be more valuable on the sparring team. So that gave him the motivation to continue.

Monday night yielded very few results. The boys stood in Simon's spare bedroom, which was refurbished into something of a mini-science lab. He had all sorts of equipment and gadgets. The boys spent what seemed like forever with Jake standing in the center of the room and Gabriel by the door with a fire extinguisher. But Jake wasn't able to generate a flame from his hands. He stood there focusing on his hands. He tried to raise his internal body temperature and focus it into his fingers. Then he snapped his fingers. Still, there was no flame.

Simon decided to call the practice short for dinner. Simon gave Jake his contact information and asked him to let him know when they could next meet. So the boys left and went to their dorm.

The following morning, Gabriel went to his kinetics class. Coach V had placed him in Kinetics 101, which was the more fundamental class. In this class, Gabriel would learn all of the basics of how to control his power.

The first class was similar to the previous classes Gabriel had had that week. It was mostly introductory. The class was held in the gymnasium arena. It was the same massively open room that Gabriel had seen earlier when he'd played indoor soccer with the sports club. However, this time he would get to see the whole thing.

Inside, Coach V explained to the class that they would be working on a very fundamental level on how to use their powers. He also explained that everyone in the kinetics class had a power that allowed him or her to manipulate the world around them.

"Now, this class will not be like your other classes," Coach explained. "Whereas your other classes are more study and knowledge, this class is a more practical skills class. You will be given tasks to accomplish, exercises to train you, and tests of endurance to grow your gift."

He started putting the class into groups. Gabriel didn't understand what they were doing or what they would be doing.

All he knew was that he was surprised that Coach V was dividing in so quickly where the other classes mostly had been introductory.

After the groups were made, Coach had the students run some laps. Then they worked on some exercises that Coach V explained to them. In the meantime, Gabriel found out the gifts of his teammates. One was able to move the air around him, and the other was the girl from the placement exam who could control water. They spent the remainder of class working on weight lifting with their abilities.

PROGRESS

The following weeks progressed smoothly. Gabriel learned so much from his classes, and his kinetics training was helping him learn how to use his telekinesis better. Not only were classes helpful, but also Gabriel found a small group of friends to spend time with, meeting Serena, Simon, and Jake regularly.

Although it started out as working together to help Jake with his fire generation, it quickly grew into a tight-knit group both for fun and to help each other. Serena, Simon, and Gabe all worked together on assignments, with Simon generally helping them out when they were stuck. Jake helped Gabriel with his kinetic training and workout regimes. But regardless of the point of their meeting, the group always seemed to have a fun time.

Every morning Gabriel awoke and readied himself for class. Mondays, Wednesdays, and Fridays he went to his academic classes. Tuesdays and Thursdays he went to Kinetics 101 for his practical training. He started a routine of practicing with his telekinesis every morning and some meditation. Both of these were the part of the training regime from Jake and Coach V.

During the first few weeks he learned to lift delicate objects with finesse. Then he learned to lift multiple objects at once.

He practiced regularly, and in a month he could easily lift heavy objects like his bed and dresser.

That morning was like every other. Gabe woke up and practiced and worked on his breathing. Then he prepared for class. When he walked out of the bathroom, he saw Jake doing push-ups beside his bed.

As he finished his final push-up, Jake said, "You know it has been two months that we've been roomies?"

Gabriel laughed and replied, "Wow, has it really?"

It seemed impossible, but in the blink of an eye two months had passed. It was almost November, and the boys had spent two months working and practicing together.

As he grabbed his books for class, Gabriel rushed for the door. Then, just remembering the text he'd gotten from Serena, Gabriel stopped and looked at Jake. "Hey, Serena said she has a show at the coffeehouse tonight. Are you going to come?" he asked Jake.

Now working on some sit-ups, Jake stopped and said, "Sure, I will head over after practice tonight."

***

That night Gabriel entered the Colombiana, the coffee shop on campus. The small shop smelled like rich coffee beans and sugar. Bulky wooden tables of various sizes and shapes filled the floor in no particular order. The far wall was covered in black chalkboard paint that was filled with chalk signatures, drawings, and even coffee specials.

Over in the corner there was a small stage made of old wood that had a coat of white paint that was in desperate need of a repainting. The stage was elevated and had small speakers on the edges. A stool stood in the center of the stage, with a guitar leaning against it.

Gabriel grabbed himself a cup of coffee and sat down beside the chalk wall. He was doodling on the wall with a piece of chalk that was on his table. He noticed that the coffeehouse was slowly filling up now that it was almost show time. Just then Jake walked into the building. He saw Gabriel against the wall, and they made eye contact. Jake pointed to the coffee bar and motioned that he was going to grab something to drink.

After a few moments of waiting, Gabriel saw Serena across the shop. She walked over to the stage and lifted the guitar before sitting on the small stool and placing the guitar on her lap. Behind her a keyboardist and a drummer set up. Serena leaned up into the microphone and introduced herself and her bandmates. "Thank you for coming out tonight, everyone."

Before the show got started, Jake slid into the seat next to Gabe. As he sat down, he told Gabe that Simon was going to come by later if he could make it.

Then Serena began to sing. Her soft, melodic voice filled the air. The whole room was encased in a warm glow, with Serena at the center. She sang songs of the beauty of creation, the sun in the warm, blue sky, and the joy of family. The warmth of her songs washed away the stress of school. It was as if when she sang there couldn't be an ounce of worry or fear.

After her last song, she stopped and put down her hands. She looked down at the ground, with eyes closed and mirrored a pose of prayer. Then she looked up and thanked the crowd. The gratefulness tone was genuine. She stepped off the stage and walked to Gabriel's table.

She sat down beside Gabriel and Jake. "So you guys came!"

"Of course we came. We're friends, aren't we?" said Jake. "That was great, by the way."

"Absolutely, that was fantastic," added Gabriel.

"Thank you," she answered in a gracious tone, nodding her head.

"I think I am going to grab a coffee, and then I need to meet up with some people to go over our set."

Gabriel stood up as she did. "Let us know next time you guys are going to be performing," he said.

"Oh, sure," she said. "We will be here again in a few weeks. But I will give you the details soon. I will see you in class, right?"

Nodding, Gabriel answered, "Oh yeah, totally."

"Great, I will see you in class then."

***

A few weeks later, the first snow of winter fell on the campus. The first week of December saw a tremendous drop in temperature. Winter was here. Seeing an opportunity for some research and study with Jake, Simon demanded the group meet to work with Jake on his pyrokinetic abilities. He had everyone meet after lunch on Saturday at the Quad.

They all arrived at the Quad with their heaviest winter coats, everyone but Jake. He was in his usual shorts and sleeveless shirt. Once Jake arrived, the group was ready to embark.

"Do you have everything?" asked Simon.

With a huff and a sigh, Jake answered, "Yeah."

"All right, let's get going!" Gabe said with a smile.

Carrying his heavy bag down the walkway, Jake noticed a young girl with brown hair and pale green eyes come zooming in from the sky. She flew in quickly and landed behind Gabriel and Jake. Her stomach growled, and she quietly stated how hungry she was as she walked away.

Jokingly, Jake asked Gabriel, "Have you ever noticed that the gifted with flight always seem to be hungry?"

Simon, not realizing it was more of a joke, answered, "I believe Dr. Ferentheil proved it was because they burn up so much energy using their gift."

Jake rolled his eyes and was about to reply, but a look from Gabriel told him it was better to let it go. The fire user was still annoyed they were missing the game over at the gym with the sports club. Simon had insisted that they must use this opportunity to train. A fresh snowfall would be the perfect setting to push Jake's limits, he'd said.

The boys and Serena walked past the Quad. The faculty tower stood in the distance like a massive mountain peak. The dormitories at their backs and the snow-covered tree line before them, they made their way toward the edges of campus. The mountains that ran past the campus were painted with snow in the distance, marking them in contrast to the deep blue sky above them. The picturesque setting made for a calm setting to practice.

Headed down the stone walkway, Gabriel asked Simon, "How's your internship been?"

"It's going all right. They have moved me around out of my old science lab. I used to work in the same laboratory as Dr. Drake, but it seems many of the scientists are being reassigned."

"Oh wow. Do you know why?" asked Gabriel.

Gabriel looked at Serena, who was nodding in interest. Then he looked at Jake and noticed that he was focused on something else. Readying himself for the test to come, Jake didn't seem to be up for chitchat at the moment. Although he was depressed about missing their sports club meeting, he was determined to make it worthwhile. This was going to be the day he made fire.

Meanwhile, Simon answered Gabriel. "I don't know what to think. One of my colleagues said it might be my gift. They know I can communicate with technology and want to keep me away from any databases that have classified materials."

"Wait, so your ability lets you actually communicate with technology?" asked Jake.

"Oh yes, very much so. For example," Simon said, looking at Gabriel, "you have a smart phone, right? I can tell that you received two calls this morning from your mom, three texts. And you have thirteen unread e-mails."

As the group arrived at a safe spot, they dropped their bags and prepared to work. They were far enough from the main campus that they were sure to not be observed. They chose an area that was far enough from the path that no one would see them by chance. Even though it wasn't against any rules to use your gift on campus, they knew they would probably get in some trouble for playing with fire in a wooded area. That was part of the reason Gabriel had two fire extinguishers in his bag.

Immediately, Simon assigned everyone a job. Serena was to set up a video recording device on a stand to document the entire session. Gabriel was put on fire patrol duty, and he pulled out the two small fire extinguishers he'd brought with him. Jake prepared himself by going through some breathing exercises that Coach V had given him. Meanwhile, Simon prepared his devices for recording Jake's body temperature, heart rate, and breathing.

They spent several hours outside that day. Simon continued to push Jake to focus and heat his body in order to create a flame. Jake worked and worked for the first hours, but the process of superheating his body burned up so many calories that he had to stop multiple times during their session to eat and drink so he could refuel.

By the time the sun began setting in the distance, Jake hadn't been successful in creating a flame. The main problem was his inability to get his body temperature high enough. Simon estimated he would need to get his hand around five hundred degrees Celsius. However, as close as he got, Jake just couldn't reach that high a temperature.

Simon decided that it might be time to wrap up and head back for dinner. However, Jake said he wanted to try once more. So, they agreed to give it one more shot. With a small snack just eaten, Jake prepped for his last try of the day. He focused as hard as he could on his hand. Like Coach V suggested, he visualized fire—warm, white, and wonderful.

Although Jake hadn't reached high enough temperatures before, Simon noticed that his gauges were showing a rapid increase in Jake's internal temperature. His readings told him it was just over four hundred degrees Celsius.

"You got it, Jake," he stated, excitedly. "Keep pushing it!"

Then he did it. He broke the five-hundred-degree Celsius barrier. At his current temperature, Simon knew he could create a flame. He looked up at Jake. "Now!" he yelled.

Immediately, Jake snapped his fingers. Instead of the small spark they were expecting, a massive eruption burst from his fingers. The rest of the youngsters were all started by the volcano-like eruption. Gabriel was so jolted that he fell to the ground and doused himself with one of the fire extinguishers. In seconds, the blazing inferno roared into the air and faded into the now dark sky. Jake dropped to the ground, shocked and startled by the flaming torrent.

Everyone stood back up and looked at each other in complete silence for several seconds. Simon was the first to react. He hopped up and down with elation. Gabriel smiled at him, shaking his head at how crazy and amazing that was. Serena seemed surprised.

"That was great, Jake. I think we are not far from getting you to where you need to be."

Jake sighed. "I nearly exploded the entire forest, though."

Without a pause, Simon answered, "Well, that is because oxygen in the air is flammable. We had the right precautions in place, and with more practice, you will prevent that."

"Congratulations, Jake," Serena said enthusiastically. "You've made some great progress."

Simon chimed in once again. "I think I know the main issue," he said, looking back and forth between Jake and Gabriel. "You two were talking about it before. Remember?"

Gabriel and Jake looked at each other with no clue what Jake was talking about. So Simon explained.

"Like you said about those with the gift of flight, they expend so much energy they are extremely hungry. Your gift expends so much energy I think you need to have a more specific diet."

"You mean I need to eat more?" asked Jake.

"Not just more, but we also need to get you on a diet that will give you energy. Foods like oatmeal and wheat grains should help. We can work out the details later."

With that the boys shook hands and congratulated each other on their success.

***

The semester ended two weeks later. After handing in his last term paper, a long essay on the origins of baptisms, Gabriel's semester was officially over. He felt he'd done well enough in his classes. Even in McManus's science class, which was probably the hardest class of them all, he felt like he'd managed a B.

The group met together, said their goodbyes, and left for their respective homes. Gabriel was picked up by his father, while Jake took a cab to the airport to meet his dad, who was on a tropical beach in the Bahamas. Although he envied Jake terribly for getting to spend Christmas on a white sandy beach, Gabriel was just glad he would get to see his family. He'd missed his sister terribly. She called him all the time, but it wasn't the same.

When his father pulled up to the school to pick Gabriel up, his sister, Leigh, was in the back seat. She was watching her favorite princess television show, *Pretty Little Ladies*, the tale of four princesses who couldn't get along and who learned the importance of being honest with your friends. Gabriel didn't understand the point of the show, but he knew his sister loved it. Also, she demanded to be called "Princess Leigh" now.

Winter break came and went quickly. To Gabriel, it was as if he'd just gotten home when he was already packing to return to SIA. He and his parents left with Leigh for the campus bright one morning in mid-January. The semester wouldn't be starting for another week, but Gabriel wanted to meet up with Jake and Simon.

FILE #8

ON THE BENCH

After Kinetics 101 was Kinetics 201, the more advanced practical class where Gabriel got to use his telekinesis. This class was taught by Coach V, who taught Kinetics 101 as well. This was probably Gabriel's favorite course, because Gabriel loved working with Coach V. He'd helped Gabriel develop his gift like he'd never thought possible.

As the days stretched into weeks, the routine of the semester became more normal to Gabriel. Likewise, the more time that passed, the more Jake grew excited. His team's sparring meet was coming up in a few weeks. The week before it, Jake couldn't talk about anything else.

That Saturday, Gabriel and the rest of the crew arrived at the arena early to get in line for the meet. Serena, Simon, and Gabriel waited for more than an hour before they got inside. They made their way to their seats and waited some more. The arena was stripped of the extra training gear, and only several sparring rings were left up, each covered in a metal cage to keep the spectators safe from any possible harm.

Although the sparring team was generally very safe, there had been cases of gifts getting out of hand. Mostly, it had been fighters who were reckless. Therefore, measures had been taken to keep the fighters and the spectators safe. Once seated, Serena asked about the cages, and Simon explained them to her.

"How dangerous is a sparring match?" she asked next.

Simon explained they were statistically safer than college football, although any full-contact sport has its dangers.

Simon explained some of the ways the sport made itself safer. The first was surrounding the ring in a protective metal fencing that was powered by a generator. This electromagnetic field protected the crowds from any chance of something inside the ring getting to them. The second was assigning referees who were trained to stop a match from getting out of hand. Some had the ability to nullify attacks or teleport if anything happened. Third was the gear. Student athletes on the sparring team wore protective clothing to help keep them safe from specific injuries.

The matches started shortly after Gabriel and his friends got settled in their seats. The large overhead screen displayed a large bracket. The names of the competitors were on the different lines connected to their opponents. Gabriel scanned the names and realized that Jake's name was not on any of the brackets.

He looked over to Simon, and over the noise of the crowd he asked, "Why isn't Jake's name on the bracket?"

"Well, he is a freshman. First-year students generally don't compete. It's considered a little too dangerous for most competitors," Simon answered as if it were obvious.

Although Gabriel and Jake had hoped that Jake would qualify because of his progress at the end of last semester, they'd known it was something of a long shot. Yes, Jake had made great strides. At the beginning of the semester he couldn't create a flame by hand, but now he was able to generate a spark. The main issue now was just keeping it safe.

"Are you all right?" Serena asked.

"I just feel bad for Jake. I know he'll be upset that he still can't compete."

She smirked. "If there is one thing I've learned about Jake, it's that he has a lot of pride. Something inside him needs to be the best. I think he'll be a little embarrassed that he can't compete."

She looked at Gabriel with a smile.

"What?" he asked, smiling back at her.

"That's probably why you two are such good friends. You both have that desire to be the best. I think the two of you push each other."

Gabriel smirked and nodded in agreement. "I think you may be right."

After several matches, Gabriel saw Jake sitting on the bench of one of the fights. The competitor in the ring was Isaac Gutierrez. He was a nimble and competent fighter. Gabriel watched him move about the ring with ease. The fight went back and forth, and several times it looked like Isaac would be defeated.

As he watched, his eyes kept moving toward Jake. He noticed how defeated Jake looked. Every once in a while, Coach V would kneel down beside Jake, his large frame crouched beside Jake as he whispered to him. Gabriel knew Coach V was telling Jake about the fight. Maybe he was asking Jake questions about what he thought, or giving Jake tips for the days Jake would be in the ring. Coach V never missed a teaching opportunity.

Several more matches started and ended. Finally, the winner was announced. The winner of the advanced singles was a boy from another school. The winner of the intermediate singles was a girl from SIA. Serena nudged Gabriel and whispered that she was Lucien's girlfriend. Then they announced the advanced doubles winners. It was a team of boys who were very impressive—they were even nicknamed the Juggernauts because they were so good.

***

A few weeks later, Gabriel was preparing for class. He moved toward his kinetic science class. Professor Dyeus was at the front, manipulating some wind to pass out papers across the room as he wrote some notes on the board. Gabriel looked at what he was writing. It was information they would be tested on for their upcoming midterms. A shock struck his heart. How could midterms be just a few weeks away already?

Dyeus was a tall man from the country of India. He had dark, black hair with just a hint of gray around his ears. He always wore bright colors with elaborate patterns from his homeland. Gabriel loved his style and often wished he could pull off such amazing outfits.

During class, Dyeus was lecturing on how telekinesis could manipulate almost any matter, with training. It could lift most light objects with ease, however, denser objects and materials were much harder to lift.

Then the professor leaned against his desk and removed his small, circular glasses. Looking around the room, he asked the class, "Why do you think this is?"

The first to answer said it was because the denser objects were heavier. He nodded slightly but still looked unsatisfied. "Anyone else?" he asked.

Gabriel answered, "Well, if you have a denser object, it requires more concentration to control, right?"

"Yes," answered Dyeus. "Can you explain that with more detail?"

At first Gabriel stuttered. Unsure of how to answer, Gabriel explained that when you were using your gift on an object, it took a lot of focus to move it. Denser objects had more material and required the user to really focus to move them.

Nodding, Dyeus stood up from where he was leaning on his desk. "True, but what I really mean is the focus aspect. When you're attempting to lift denser objects, it requires more focus, right?"

The class nodded in agreement.

Dyeus continued, "So you have to really believe you can lift that object when you are attempting to do so. It requires you to put your heart and soul into it. If you are going to try and manipulate some massive structure or object, you'd better believe with all your heart that you can do it. Otherwise, you will be destined to fail."

The class looked somewhat confused. Dyeus sighed and waved his hand in circles as if he were trying to make the word come to him. "I believe the word is faith. You have to believe in what you're doing, otherwise it's doomed to fail."

Gabriel nodded. His old soccer coaches had instilled in them the same idea. Without faith in the team, the cause, and the players, his coach would tell them, they could not compete. They had to trust in their abilities.

At the end of class, Gabriel began collecting all of his belongings. He noticed one of the students go up to Professor Dyeus. It looked as if he were asking him something urgent. Dyeus shook his head and said something harsh. Whatever the student was asking him, Dyeus didn't want to hear it. The student walked back to his friend and sat down.

On the way out of the classroom, Gabriel was behind the student who'd approached Dyeus. The student was complaining to his friend as they walked.

"I can't believe he was being so rude. I mean, I was just asking for an extension," said the first boy.

His friend responded, "You didn't honestly tell him what you told me, did you?"

"Of course I did. It was the truth. I was just in my room working on Friday, and then next thing I know, I was waking up on my floor, and it was Monday."

"You seriously expect your professor to believe you were abducted or something?" asked the friend, unkindly.

The first boy sighed and said, "My roommate told me that I was nowhere to be found all weekend, but next thing you know I am back on Monday."

As they exited the classroom, the friend looked over his shoulder. Gabriel pretended he was looking at his books. Once the friend believed Gabriel wasn't eavesdropping, he said, "Listen man. I believe you. I don't know if I buy the abduction part. But you can't expect a teacher to believe you were kidnapped all weekend and then give you a week extension on your paper. It just isn't going to happen."

"I guess you're right," said the first boy. "I guess I'm going to just have to finish as much as I can and turn it in on Friday."

Gabriel walked toward the gymnasium, thinking how odd that had been. He found it so weird that anyone would make up such a story to get out of a paper. If you were going to try and get out of an assignment, at least make the excuse somewhat believable.

Before he headed to his next class, Gabriel stopped at a small food truck that had amazing fish tacos that Gabriel couldn't pass up. After his tenth taco, he darted off to class, making it to the gym quickly despite the taco detour. Wiping some crumbs from his face, he entered the stone building, Unlike last year, Gabriel didn't feel as lost inside the gymnasium. Its enormous size and confusing design made it hard to maneuver, but this semester he felt more comfortable with the layout.

In Kinetics 201, Gabriel went through his normal routines. Coach usually gave them some warm-up activities to work on as a small group. This week, it was moving objects while blindfolded. After almost fifteen minutes of trying to move a pencil without looking at it, Gabriel and the class met up by Coach V.

As usual, they were all broken up into small groups and given their assignments. He said, "Remember; you will be having tests this semester. Last year you were graded on a pass/fail system. This semester you will be given a practical exam where you will be given a set of objectives to complete. You will be graded on how well you complete them."

A hand shot up, and a voice asked, "Are these exercises practice for the midterm?"

"Yes, yes, they are. You'll be working on some tasks that should help you prepare for the midterms, all right? Any more questions?"

When no more questions were asked, Coach V sent them on their way. He stayed back with Gabriel, a boy named Omar, and Zoey. He looked at Gabriel and the rest of them. "So, guys, we've been working on defensive techniques this semester. I want you all to get into your positions and keep working on your defensive shielding. Each of you has made good progress in creating defensive barriers, but today we're going to take it to the next level. Sound good?" asked Coach V.

The students all nodded.

Coach put them into a circle and training started with Gabriel. He had Omar put his hand forward, and then Gabriel worked on repelling it with his telekinesis. At first it was hard to focus. As Coach V had told him, shielding yourself with telekinesis was very difficult. It required focusing your energy into a cocoon around you. Coach V had told Gabriel to think about a river of water flowing away from him, to think about the object he wanted to repel floating away from him.

Gabriel hadn't had success when they'd first started, but today he was doing much better. Omar's outstretched hand could not move close to Gabriel. It was as if there were an invisible barrier around Gabriel. However, the shield wasn't completely invisible. Small ripples, almost like wafting steam, could be seen in the air around him.

Then they gave Gabriel a break and let Zoey go. Gabriel tried to push his hand toward Zoey. She pushed him back on her first try. Likewise, Omar had no trouble repelling Zoey's hand with his gravity manipulation.

Next, Coach V had them working on throwing punches at each other. For safety's sake, Coach had them make sure not to aim directly. Instead, they just aimed for the space in front of their opponent. As Omar threw his first punch at Gabriel, Gabriel had to react very quickly. He just barely caught the punch with his mind. Omar's hand hovered there, unable to move any closer. Omar's eyes widened in shock. Initially, he'd expected to get through Gabriel's defenses.

Afterward, Omar gave Gabriel a hardy high-five for his success. They repeated the process several more times that lesson and even more times that week. The coach continued to push Gabriel in his shielding and defensive capabilities. Although the work was hard, Gabriel developed more and more with Coach V's training.

FILE #9

STRANGER

On Monday morning, many classes were replaced with workshops. Recruiters were on campus, speaking about the various jobs for gifted individuals. In Gabriel's class, they had a tall woman with glasses and a dark blue skirt. Those that weren't captivated by her beauty, were captivated by her grace and poise. She explained that this was a yearly event, and that they would discuss many of the career options available in the gifted program.

She showed them statistics from businesses that were growing around the world. The first was Kinegetics Energy Co., a large company that hired various gifteds to power homes, towns, and even cities. Their company had grown steadily since their start years ago.

The next was Pharis International. This company was in charge of helping find jobs for gifted individuals in companies where they could be of the most use. They had grown even more than Kinegetics. After that, she showed them one of the agencies that was hiring, the Fitz-Simmons Agency. Agencies were facilities that were sponsored by the government to help with situations that fell out of the reach of the police and army. Located outside of Washington, D.C., with an impressive record for solving everything from natural disasters to terrorist threats. Fitz-Simmons was one of the most well-known agencies.

The rest of the class continued with a discussion on various jobs, companies, and agencies. The recruiter ended with a ten-minute question-and-answer time for students to ask any unanswered questions they might still have.

Gabriel and Jake had planned on meeting up for lunch that afternoon in between classes. They'd decided to meet at the campus café for some sandwiches and then head back to class. Gabriel met Jake outside the café, glued to his phone. He was reading something about the arena, the gifted fighting league with the most powerful gifted fighters in the world. Gabriel got the feeling Jake wanted to join the arena when he was older.

"Hey," Gabriel said, but there was no reply—Jake was completely oblivious. So, using his telekinesis, Gabriel pulled the device from Jake's hands. It zipped into Gabriel's clutches, and he spun it menacingly.

Jake's eyes locked on Gabriel and then onto his phone. "Not funny, man," he said. "I was reading an article about the fight between Valentino Valdez and Killian Masterson next week."

As Gabriel returned Jake's device, he replied, "That's awesome. Why don't we grab lunch, and you can tell me about it?"

The boys grabbed some sandwiches and found a spot to sit. Jake was mid-sentence when he spied two young ladies sitting behind them. Instantly, Gabriel knew what he was up to. Jake leaned back and asked the young lady to his right if she had any ketchup on her table. Both of the girls smiled and said no.

"Wow, that's an interesting eye color you have there," he said in his most silky-smooth voice. The voice he used was a deeper version of his normal voice, but he enunciated more clearly and put extra emphasis on some words. Gabriel rolled his eyes.

The brunette laughed and said, "Thank you." Her eyes were a deep shade of purple with flecks of dark blue throughout.

They were big and full of life. Honestly, Gabriel couldn't lie—she did have beautiful eyes, but this was just Jake's go-to line for opening conversations with girls.

"Are you two gifteds?" Jake asked next.

"I can shapeshift, but my friend here has an immunity to cold," she answered. "What about you boys?"

After the boys answered, they introduced themselves to each other and began talking. The shyer girl was Sara. She was in her second year and was a Grade C. She had brown hair, large, thick glasses, and was very short. Her mousy appearance was mirrored in her personality—calm, quiet, and reserved, very unlike her friend.

Her friend the shapeshifter was tall, with an athletic build. Her hair was blond with rainbow colors streaked throughout, and she was loud and talkative. Gabriel recognized her—her face was on various posters around campus—as the leader of the student council. Her name was Gina, and she was a Grade A gifted, one of the top students on campus.

The boys ate their sandwiches as they chatted with the girls. They compared classes, teachers, and experiences. For the most part, they had similar classes, but Gina was in a very different program. Her ability was not one that was sought by the main companies, but she was interested in working for one of the big agencies.

She told the boys she wanted to be an undercover agent. She loved the idea of danger and the thrill of the unknown. Gabriel's eyes widened. He was surprised that she was such a thrill-seeker.

Gabriel finished his lunch first. He looked at the clock and thought about how long it would take him to get to class. He shrugged his shoulders—he would be able to stay for a few more minutes. Jake spent the rest of their lunch telling stories about being on the sparring team, about matches he'd seen and others he'd fought in. Gabriel wondered how much was completely accurate, considering he couldn't compete.

Then the mousy-looking girl asked Gabriel what he wanted to do when he finished school. He looked at her with a shock of dread. He hadn't really decided. He knew he wanted to work with one of the gifted-based groups around the world, but he'd never decided exactly which one or what field.

"Honestly, I'm not sure." There was a pause, then he added, "I think I'd like to work in law enforcement. My dad is a cop, and that's something I have always thought I would enjoy."

Gina shook her head and clicked her tongue. "You should join an agency. They're the ones really make a change for the better."

Unnerved by her attitude, Gabriel made a face that showed he was unimpressed with her answer. "I've read they have a lot of red tape because they're government agencies. I wrote a paper in my history class last semester about it. Sometimes they can't even get to places and help because the United Nations can't grant them the rights."

Gina looked shocked. "Well, still. Policemen have the same problem. If their commander says no, they can't do anything to help."

Gabriel nodded. "Yeah, true. Maybe I'll figure out what I want to do this year. Who knows?"

Gina looked unimpressed. She made an ever-so-slight shake of her head. Gabriel leaned back and rolled his eyes. He looked at Jake and gave him a this-girl-is-crazy look. Jake smirked and went back to looking at Sara. Gabriel wasn't the combative type, but Gina was pushing him.

"What do you want to do, Sara?" Jake asked, trying to change the subject.

"Oh, me? I want to be a teacher. Maybe high school, but I would love to work at a place like this," she said, indicating the campus of SIA. "I think what they're doing here is amazing."

Gabriel nodded his head in unison with Jake.

Then Gina spoke up again. "Are you ready for your end-of-year practical exams?" she asked.

Jake said jokingly, "We haven't even had midterms yet. Why are you getting ready for those?"

"You have to be ready for them. Every year we have end-of-year exams. They're practical exams with your gifts. If you can't complete them, you aren't able to move on to more advanced studies and grade up."

"Grade up?" asked Gabriel in a quizzical tone.

Annoyed by his question, Gina answered, "Grade up is when you move from a grade. Like from Grade A to S."

Gabriel nodded and then stopped. "Grade S? There is a grade above A?"

"Oh, yeah," she said in a tone of superiority. She brushed her hair back as she spoke. "Grade S is for very advanced gifted, the ones you see on the news, saving people from earthquakes or tornadoes. They're the strongest gifteds in the world."

Gabriel looked shocked but interested. "Wow, I didn't even know that."

"Well, now you do," Gina answered in an abrasive tone.

Gabriel had had enough with her tone, her attitude, and her grandiose mentality. He stood up and was about to say something, but Jake grabbed his tray. In perfect timing, Jake said, "Let me grab the trays, man. It's cool."

Gina didn't even seem to realize Gabriel's exasperation. "Fine," Gabriel said to Jake. "I have to get to class, anyway."

Jake grabbed the trays and dropped them off. Gabriel walked out, and Jake followed. Once out of sight of Gina, Gabriel looked at Jake.

"What was that girl's problem?" he asked.

"Eh, who knows, man? Just one of those people who thinks they know better than everyone else."

"How can she act like that?" Gabriel asked. "We're all people, right?"

"Hey, I know that, and you know that. But not everyone is as awesome as us," Jake said with a smile.

After a few minutes of walking, Gabriel thought about what Jake had done. He realized that Jake had seamlessly known what had been wrong and reacted. Only a real friend would have done what he'd done.

As they passed the Student Union Building, Gabriel said to Jake without looking, "Thanks for catching me when I was about to lose my temper."

"Hey, what are friends for, my man?"

That was where the boys split up. Jake went off to one of his practices. The team held multiple practices each day, and the teammates had to go to one a day. Not being a morning person, Jake always went to the later ones. Gabriel, meanwhile, had to head toward the Science Building for his own class.

Gabriel was still waving to Jake when there was a *clank* sound, followed by a throbbing pain in his chest and jaw. A burning sensation rushed to Gabriel's face. His vision blurred, and he shook uncontrollably. His legs turned to mush below him, and he stumbled to the ground. The rough concrete scraped his hands as he landed.

Slowly, the deafening ring in his ears died down. Soon the sounds of the school could be heard again—the patter of feet on the concrete, the chatter of a girl on the phone, and the metallic thud of nearby doors closing. Gabriel rose to his knees. His eyes fluttered up and down, unable to focus.

Wobbly legs made their way to a standing position. Before him, he expected to see a metal pole or a wall, but there were neither. Instead, there stood a man. Gabriel shook his head, blinked thirty or forty times, and peered again. How could it be? Gabriel's eyes weren't playing tricks on him, and he wasn't under some sort of concussion symptom. There really was a man before him who had knocked him over.

The man was wrapped in a suit made of the finest silk and black as the night, with shoes shined and as flashy as the moon's reflection, wearing black gloves made of rich leather that covered his hands. His suit seemed unnaturally tight as his bulky physique stretched the fibers of the material to their limits. His muscular frame barely fit inside his suit.

Gabriel couldn't believe it. The man was completely unfazed by Gabriel's unintended assault on him. When his eyes focused, Gabriel realized the man wasn't even aware of what had happened. He was staring at his large phone. Whether he was oblivious or too intent, Gabriel couldn't tell.

As Gabriel took a step toward the man, a sharp pain stabbed at his chest. "Going to feel that in the morning," he said to himself. Gabriel coughed to get the man's attention, but still he didn't move.

"Sir, I am sorry. I didn't mean to run into you."

The stout man stood motionless, as if mimicking a statue. He was rigid, and Gabriel's eyes widened as he realized just how abnormally muscular the man was. Where a neck should have been, the man seemed to go from head to massively thick shoulders. He wore sunglasses on top of his head over a bleach-blond Mohawk.

Gabriel rounded to look at his face and make a formal apology. Then he saw the stony face before him. The man's nose and chin looked like they were carved from granite, all sharp lines and angles.

"Uh, sir, are you all right?" Gabriel asked.

The man looked at Gabriel and made no facial expression. Two silvery steel eyes bored into him. Unable to look away, Gabriel remained paralyzed.

"You know where the dormitories are, kid?" the man with the Mohawk asked.

"They're that way," Gabriel answered, pointing to his right.

"Thanks," the man said, and he started walking off in that direction.

Gabriel turned away, clenching his sore jaw. He moved his mouth up and down, attempting to work out the soreness. He wondered what a man—who looked clearly as if he were too old to be a student—would be doing on campus. But then it hit him—he was going to be late. Thunderously, Gabriel's' steps slammed down on the pavement, scratching against the concrete as he moved as quickly as he could through the crowds coming and going to classes. Nearby, the speedster named Eames zoomed through the crowds like lightning. A tinge of jealousy hit Gabriel.

Once in the building, the job of moving quickly became even harder. The crowds had thickened and there was less space to move in the confined quarters. With nimble feet and a little good fortune, Gabriel snuck into the room just as the professor was getting to the front. Amazingly, the professor's back was turned, and Gabriel grabbed a seat before he noticed.

The lecture began quickly. First, the teacher gave a summary of their previous lecture, and then, just as he was explaining that they had a guest lecturer, the side door swung open. A small figure stood in the doorway, and his dwindled frame and haggard expression gave him away immediately. It was Dr. Drake, the leading researcher on campus.

As Gabriel watched Dr. Drake approached the podium, he studied him intently. Drake had long, white hair combed back over his head and was wearing a pair of dark goggles around his neck as if he'd just finished an experiment and taken them off right before walking into the room. His face and hands were covered in age spots. His weak and withered frame shook slightly as he walked. He wore a black lab coat, fastened tightly all the way up to his neck. Gabriel got a chill running up his spine. Maybe it was the room—or maybe it was the cold demeanor that Drake had given off when he'd entered the room.

Dr. Drake stood before the class of students and looked around to gauge their pursuit of knowledge. There were students who were smart, students who were geniuses, and then there was a level beyond that. Dr. Drake was even above that level. Drake approached the podium and looked from side to side at the rows of students in the room. While most professors and scientists appreciated students and those who were learning, Drake actually looked down on anyone who was less intelligent than him.

"Welcome," he started, almost gritting as he said it. "I am Dr. Drake, and I am so glad you are here today."

Gabriel noticed Dr. Drake winced when he said that. Drake continued.

"As you most likely know, I am the lead scientist on campus. I am also a gifted, like many of you here—well, not quite like you," he said, almost sneering at the class. "My gift is called hypercognition, hyper meaning rapid speed and cognition meaning my brain power. It allows my brain to process at speeds faster than·any other person on the planet, to think at an amazing rate."

He looked at the class as if he were expecting them to clap at his amazing gift. When no applause came, he decided to continue. "My team and I have been exploring the progression of gifts for years now. Today we will be discussing the breakthroughs I have accomplished."

Dr. Drake went through some of his research, explaining the way gifts developed in a person. He detailed how the gamma rays from the sun changed as they passed through Venus' atmosphere, how they warped, and how these rays only hit earth when Venus was in between earth and the sun—that was why gifteds only came around every so often.

Then another man entered the room, the large, muscular man with the blond Mohawk who Gabriel had run into. He walked in and stood in the corner, causing Dr. Drake to stop and turn around. The man with the hulking form made eye contact with Drake and shook his head as if signaling that something wasn't right. Dr. Drake dropped his head as if disappointed, but he didn't stop long. His exchange with the man was only about a second, and then, without hesitation, Drake turned and continued.

He explained some of his newer findings, stating that he believed that—with some of the mineral composition of Venus—they might even be able to use stones and minerals to give more people gifts. One unique mineral, which he called Venisium, could give anyone gifts.

The man with the Mohawk remained in the far corner of the room and didn't move. At times, Gabriel thought he was a metal statue, he was so still. At the end of his lecture, Drake left the podium without saying much else. He walked to the man with the Mohawk, and they exited through the side door.

After class, Gabriel headed toward his dorm room. He had a paper due next week, and he wanted to get some work done on it before it got late. He figured once Jake got back from his team practice, there would be no chance of getting any work done, so he headed toward the library.

Just as he was able to see the library in the distance, he noticed a flicker of red out of the corner of his eye. He turned and saw Serena rush up beside him, looking excited. Gabriel's own face lit up, and he smiled at her. She grabbed his arm and showed him a flier.

"Oh great," he said when he read it.

She had handed him a tan piece of paper with a simple, bold print, that announced she would be singing at the Colombiana again that weekend. It had the times and the name of Serena's small band.

"So, you guys are The Gingers now?" asked Gabriel, referring to the band name.

"Yeah, because I am a redhead and so is Jimmy the guitarist," she answered with a matter-of-fact tone.

"But the other two are brunettes, so why not The Brunettes?" asked Gabriel, sarcastic.

"Well, The Gingers is shorter and catchier, of course," she answered back.

"If you say so." He faked a sigh of annoyance.

"Whatever. Will you be there?" she asked.

"Oh yeah, this sounds awesome. I will get the guys together and see you there."

"Thanks, it means a lot that you'll be there."

"Of course," he said with a smile.

"I need to run to my next class. We're having a scavenger hunt, and we have to use our gifts to find all the clues."

She began running in the opposite direction. Gabriel lingered for a moment, staring off into the distance.

***

That evening, Gabriel went to bed after watching television with Jake. He rolled over in his bed, falling deeper into unconsciousness, where he was plagued with dreams. No, not dreams, nightmares. He stood in a room that looked similar to his dorm room but was cleaner in every way.

Gabriel noticed that he had a glass and a plate in his hands. The glass was clear, with a unique, pink rim and around the bottom were flowers painted along a patch of grass. The plate was yellow with bright, orange flowers. On the plate appeared to be the remains of a midnight snack. Before him was a sink in a small kitchenette.

He took a step toward the sink. Suddenly, a massive arm wrapped around his neck. The arm was thick, but something was different about it. Instead of the normal softness of skin, it had the hard coldness of metal. He kicked and punched, and the contact made a metallic *ping* of vibration.

Fear began to grip him as he failed to fight off the villain. His eyes darted left and right, panic broke over him, and his mind raced. He didn't understand what was happening, and a million things rushed through his mind. The pinching of the man's arm around his neck made it hard to breathe. His lungs burned; his throat was on fire. There was a fading around the edges of his vision and twinkles of light formed in the distance.

Just as everything started to go dark, he saw something—in the corner, there was a mirror where he could see himself. It wasn't himself he saw. He wasn't Gabriel Green—instead, he saw someone else where he was standing. He was a girl with red hair, tall and lean. Behind her stood a man with a blond Mohawk, in a dark black suit, who held her in his bear-like arms.

Looking down, Gabriel—or whoever he was—saw the broken glass that he'd dropped. Next to it was the plate, broken cleanly in two. He saw the flowers on the plate, and then everything faded to black.

FILE #10

MISSING

That morning Gabriel awoke with a splitting headache. There was a piercing pain that ran from his forehead to the top of his neck. The pain in his head was only outdone by the sharp sting he got when he looked at the window and saw the sunlight. He rolled over with a whine and a groan. The pain kept pounding away like a drumbeat. The silence helped, seeming to slow the throbbing, that was, until Jake's alarm went off.

Immediately the shooting pain returned to his head, cracking his brain in two. Or at least it felt that way. Gabriel heard Jake arise. He heard the thud of two feet hitting the floor.

"You all right?" asked Jake. "You are usually already awake and eating when I get up."

"My head is killing me," Gabriel answered. "I think it is going to explode."

Jake made a thinking sound as if he wasn't sure. "Hmm, maybe you are getting sick. Want some medicine?"

"We have some headache stuff in the bathroom."

Jake returned a few seconds later with a bottle and a glass of water. Gabriel took the medicine and closed his eyes. Within ten minutes, he felt the pain start to subside. When Gabriel sat up, he blinked his eyes. It seemed hard to focus his eyes. Although the pain that felt like an axe driving into his skull was gone, he still felt less than perfect.

He looked over at his alarm clock on the nightstand. It was later than he'd realized, so he attempted to get up and get ready for class, but it was very difficult. Whereas he normally took less than an hour to get ready, it took him almost twice as long today. Repeatedly, he had to brace himself to regain his balance. And on one occasion, he had to grab the bathroom sink and thought he was going to vomit all over the bathroom.

Gabriel went to his first class where they were continuing to practice kinetic shielding. By the time he made it to class, the medicine was working, and his migraine was all but gone. At first, he thought he might tell Coach V that he was sick and go back to his room, but he was feeling so much better now.

Despite the grogginess that Gabriel had experienced that morning, he was doing surprisingly well. Early on, he fumbled, unable to deflect the dodgeballs that his partner tossed at him. However, after almost half an hour, he was doing much better and could deflect the dodgeball when his partner chucked it at him full force.

Gabriel stopped repeatedly during his training to take water breaks. He kept experiencing a shortness of breath as if he was in need of a tall glass of water or something. It felt like his old asthma attacks when he'd been younger. He hoped he wouldn't need to see the nurse, but he decided to take it easy the rest of class.

After class, Gabriel met up with the guys at Simon's dorm room where they were working on something with Jake. Jake was hooked up with all kinds of wires and even wore a helmet over his head. Gabriel could tell they were in the thick of some sort of experiment concerning Jake's gift. He couldn't tell what it was, but he knew it was something big.

"What are you guys working on?" asked Gabriel.

Simon was zipping around the floor on his rolling chair. While he slid from one computer to another, he said, "Can't talk now, Green. We are so close to a breakthrough."

"Are you guys going to come to Serena's thing tonight?" Gabriel asked.

"I'm sorry, but we are too busy tonight. Tell her we will hang out tomorrow."

So, with nothing to do and no one to be with, Gabriel sauntered off to the coffeehouse. The show wasn't for another hour, but he didn't have anything better to do.

As usual, the Colombiana had the lights on the dimmest setting possible. Gabriel grabbed his coffee and sat at a chair that didn't match the table where it had been placed. He looked at the wall beside him, which was covered in a chalk-drawn coffee-related graffiti.

Before he even realized it, half an hour had passed. Gabriel looked around at the baristas behind the coffee bar. They were all looking nervous and anxious. Gabriel noticed that one of them was on the phone while two others were in a heated conversation near the back door. Two more were trying to fill all the coffee orders.

Then the staff member who had been on the phone walked over and said something to the two who were in the heated discussion. She looked upset, but she spoke very quickly. Then she walked up to the front and grabbed a sign. Then she walked past Gabriel to the small stage and placed a small sign on the stool that sat there.

Gabriel craned his neck to see what the sign said. It read Canceled.

She stepped over to the microphone and tapped it. It made a booming noise. "Hey, guys, we are going to be canceling the show tonight. The Gingers will not be able to perform tonight. Sorry."

Gabriel was confused. He tried to catch the barista as she walked back to the coffee area, but she said she was too busy to talk. She had to return to the ordering station to handle the long line that was massing at the front.

Since he wasn't feeling much better, Gabriel decided to call it a day and get back home. He got to his room, crawled in bed, and dozed off immediately. He slept so hard that he didn't even notice Jake come in late that night, and thankfully he woke up the next morning feeling much better.

Classes went by quickly and smoothly. However, he didn't see Serena in class. He did run into her friend Ruth, who played in Serena's band. He asked her where Serena was after class. She explained to Gabriel that she hadn't seen her yesterday. They had been supposed to meet for a preshow rehearsal, but Serena hadn't shown up.

"That's unlike her," said Gabriel.

"Very," answered Ruth. "We tried to call her, but she didn't answer. We couldn't find her or reach her, so we called the Colombiana before the show and told them to cancel the show because we had a sick member."

"Oh, ok," Gabriel said. "I was there when they got the call, I think, at least."

She turned around to head out of the classroom, but then she stopped and turned around. "Wait," she said.

"What?"

"You hang out with her almost as much as I do. Can you give her this?" she asked.

"Sure, what is it?" Gabriel asked confused.

"It's an assignment from one of our classes. She wasn't there so my professor gave it to me to give to her."

"All right."

"I have a copy of the assignment, but you take this one. If I see her first, I will give her mine to copy. If you see her first, give her that one, all right?" Ruth said, more telling than asking.

Somewhat intimidated, Gabriel nodded in reply.

After another full day, Gabriel made plans to meet up with the guys at Simon's dorm again. Gabriel opened the door and entered. He heard some chatter in the next room, which was Simon's science lab. When Gabriel entered, Jake was jumping up and down, and Simon was smiling from ear to ear. Gabriel could tell something very important had happened.

When the boys saw him, Jake bounded over to Gabriel as if he could fly. He landed with a thud in front of Gabriel and screamed, "I did it!"

"What did you do," Gabriel said, his eyes as wide as saucers.

"I can finally start to make fire," Jake answered with an overly enthused tone.

Gabriel's eyes widened even more, and he exclaimed, "That's awesome!"

Simon walked over with a pen over his ear and his glasses in his hands. He was wiping them with his shirt. "It was easy, once we figured out the proper trigger for his sparks."

"Yeah, now you can make sparks anytime?" asked Gabriel.

Jake was still hopping. "Yeah, as long as I can burning focus. Thanks to Simon, we perfected the technique, temperature, and timing."

The boys celebrated by ordering the largest pizza they could get from the pizzeria. They had soda, junk food, and more pizza than was advisable. As they sat around Simon's living room, Gabriel felt like something was missing. He couldn't put his finger on it, but he knew something was different. Between bites of his pizza, it hit him: Serena wasn't celebrating with them. She was involved as much as Gabriel was in working with Jake.

"Hey," Gabriel asked. "Have you guys seen Serena?"

Simon swallowed a large piece and looked perplexed for a moment. Jake stopped jumping on the couch and stood still. Both of them shook their heads in reply. Neither had seen Serena.

"She wasn't at the café the other night for her performance. They ended up having to cancel."

"I heard about that," stated Jake. "One of her band members works out at the gym in the afternoons. He told me she didn't show up for rehearsal, and so they had to cancel on them."

"Yeah, they haven't seen her either," Gabriel said.

"I wonder if she's sick," stated Simon very matter-of-factly.

Gabriel nodded. "Yeah, she must be. I have an assignment for her. I'll bring it by her dorm and drop it off for her."

So, Gabriel brought over the assignment that evening while the other boys remained at Simon's eating pizza to their hearts' content. Gabriel made his way to the girl's dorm building. He stopped at the front desk. At the front desk sat a tall girl with dark skin and braided hair. She was flipping through a magazine as Gabriel approached. He recognized her immediately.

"Hey, Alaya, right?" he asked.

"Yeah," she said with a slight southwestern accent.

After the pleasantries, Gabriel explained that he had an assignment for Serena. He just wanted to drop it off for her.

"Sure, just let me drop the barrier I have up so you can go upstairs."

Gabriel looked confused. "You have a force field up there?"

"Yeah, they let me use it when I am on staff. But it isn't always like that."

Alaya stood up. "Let me show you," she said. As she focused her gift, Gabriel noticed her eyes change a bright shade of orange. Immediately, there was a burst of blue light coming from the upstairs corridor. Then it disappeared.

Alaya's eyes returned to normal. She looked at Gabriel and said, "You're good to go. Her room is second floor, fourth room on your right."

Gabriel rushed upstairs, noticing a smell in the air. Where the boys' dorm had a strong smell of sweat and old food, the girls' dorm smelled of flowers and fruit. The sweet smell entered his nostrils and reminded him of the scented candles his mother loved so much.

Once upstairs, Gabriel found the second floor and entered the landing. He counted the doors until he came to the fourth one, where he knocked with a quick rap. He waited for several seconds. Nothing happened. With three more quick knocks, he expected someone to answer.

Realizing maybe she was unwilling to come to the door, he decided to call out to her.

"Hey, Serena, it's Gabriel. I have your assignment from Ruth."

Again, he waited at the door. His chest started to feel tight. A rushing feeling moved through his heart when he heard a creaking sound. But his stomach immediately dropped when he realized it wasn't Serena's door but the neighbor's door. Two girls walked out. Before they got more than a few steps away, Gabriel called out to them.

"Hey, have you seen Serena, the girl who lives here?" Gabriel asked with a slight plea in his voice.

They stopped and looked at each other. The girl on the right was tall and thin, with a large nose and paper-thin eyebrows. Her friend, however, was short with bushy eyebrows and bright-red lipstick. The shorter girl looked from her friend with the sharp features to Gabriel. She shook her head and told Gabriel they hadn't seen her in a few days.

Realizing that if she was sick, he should at least leave the assignment, so Gabriel bent down and put the paper to the floor. He slid the sheet of paper under the door. When he readjusted his right foot, he started to lose his balance. Instinctively, he grabbed the door handle and caught himself. It spun in his hand with a loud click and swung open. Losing his grip as the door opened, Gabriel fell to the floor on all fours, kneeling in the doorway.

He stood there staring into an empty room. He immediately covered his eyes with a hand. He apologized several times, but heard no response. Then he peaked one eye through his fingers. No one was there. Then he looked around. In many ways the room was similar to Gabriel's room. Unlike Gabriel's room, there was only one bed. Gabriel didn't know how or why, but

Serena didn't have a roommate. It was rather tidy in the room, and it smelled of oranges.

As Gabriel made his way to his feet, he noticed something. There was a glass on the ground, shattered into pieces. Beside it was a broken plate. Taking two steps toward it, his heart started to race, thumping harder and harder. A strange fuzzy feeling came over his mind, as if this wasn't real. Or maybe something else.

When he saw the plate, everything came crashing down like glass shattering in his brain. On the plate, there was a flower pattern he knew. It was his dream. He'd completely forgotten about the dream until this very second. The glass too. He'd seen both of them in the dream he'd had. But that morning he'd woken up with such a pounding headache, he didn't remember.

Then the rest of the dream came rushing over him like a flood. He recalled the girl he saw. She had red hair, and then he realized who it was. The dream was Serena. How could he have dreamed all of this when it seemed to happen?

"Wait," Gabriel said with a shock.

At that moment it was like lightning struck him. Every part of his body shook. His forehead dripped with a layer of sweat. It was at that moment, with shaking hands and pounding heart, that he realized the last part of the dream. Someone with a black suit and a blond Mohawk was holding Serena. He must have knocked her out. That was when everything in the dream went black.

But this couldn't be. How could this be real? This was all too much. Things like this didn't really happen. Did they?

FILE #11

TAKEN

Standing there, Gabriel's hands shook uncontrollably. His legs felt wobbly. They were like liquid, and his body sunk to the ground. Kneeling on the floor beside the broken plate and glass, Gabriel tried to catch up to his racing mind. However, he was too paralyzed from shock to do anything. He was frozen, immobile.

Just then, it hit him. A voice in his head told him, "Nothing is ever solved by standing still." He recognized the voice. It was his father. A calm came to his mind that had been, up until that point, running like a scared rabbit. He found the ability to stand once again. Although his knees were still knocking, he stood up.

Again, his father's voice came to him. He remembered what his father told him when he was younger and unable to solve a problem. Gabriel's father would tell him to calm down, breathe deep, and figure out what he could do next.

Gabriel asked himself, "What can I do next?"

Gabriel looked around the room. He didn't see anything around the room that helped. There were no other items that seemed out of place. Gabriel thought about fingerprints, but he didn't even have a clue about how to find those. So, what was next?

Within a moment, he decided he needed to talk this over with his friends. They could help.

After sprinting down the campus, Gabriel arrived at Simon's room. He burst through the door like a whirlwind. Both Jake and Simon were on the sofa playing a video game on Simon's large television. They turned to see the sight of a sweat-covered Gabriel at that door. His eyes were bloodshot, and his mouth was agape. He was panting heavily, almost wheezing.

"What's wrong?" asked Jake, standing up and dropping the controller.

Simon walked over to him with several quick strides. Gabriel sat down at the nearest seat, as Simon handed him a bottle of water. "Here," Simon said.

Gabriel began to explain the situation to Jake and Simon, telling them how he'd ended up at Serena's, and then he told them about how he'd accidentally got into her room.

Simon interjected that he thought it was Gabriel's telekinesis instinctively acting to open the door. In a voice that dripped with patronizing intelligence, Simon said, "I've heard of gifts acting in unique cases like that. Usually they are to save or protect the user. However, it isn't farfetched to believe your gift acted subconsciously upon your desire to see Serena."

Gabriel continued without addressing Simon's statement. He thought that the door could have been unlocked what he saw. He told them what he'd seen and about the dream he had the other night. Gabriel explained that the items were exactly like the dream.

"What do you think it all means?" asked Gabriel after several seconds of silence.

Simon didn't answer. His eyebrows were furrowed and narrow. He placed his hand under his chin, rubbing his thumb and index finger against it. Gabriel could tell he was listening, but so focused on something that he didn't answer.

Jake blurted out immediately, "I think you are just stressed, man."

Gabriel didn't reply. He looked back at Jake questioningly.

Seeing his look, Jake explained his thought. "I think you are stressed about your finals coming up and your first year almost being done at school. You are obviously just not handling the stress well."

Gabriel nodded his head for a few seconds. *Maybe he's right*, he thought. However, he didn't say it out loud. Meanwhile, Simon still looked worried. His eyes were so focused it looked like he might burn a hole in the carpet where he was staring.

There was an odd tension in the air. Jake, who was always one to speak his mind, felt odd after his comment. He knew it was somewhat harsh, but Jake always had a problem when it came to thinking first and then talking. So, he tried to switch things up by looking at Simon. "What do you think, Simon?" Jake asked.

Simon looked confused for a second. Like he was being awoken from a daydream, his eyes snapped into focus. Then he looked from Jake to Gabriel several times. Slowly, his confused expression changed to his normal one. However, he started stuttering and stammering, unsure of what to say. Gabriel wondered if he didn't want to say what he was really thinking and was trying to come up with something else.

Simon coughed into his hands. His mousey voice said, "Honestly, this sounds quite odd. I've only known you a few months, but you don't seem like the person to make something like this up."

Gabriel nodded in agreement.

"If something like this is going on, we should make a deal. If anyone of us is in trouble, we will let the others know immediately. We send a message to each other," added Simon.

"Like what?" asked Jake with a snarky tone.

"Some sort of SOS?" asked Gabriel.

"SOS, what's that stand for?" asked Jake. But in a mocking voice he asked, "Simon, our savior?"

Gabriel smirked and laughed. "No, it is a distress term that ships used to use. It means save our ship or something."

"That's not bad," said Simon. "Simon, our savior. It would be something only we understand."

"All right, so if we get into trouble, see anything odd, or need help, we message each other 'Simon, our savior,' and the rest of us go help immediately," added Gabriel.

Then Simon had an idea. He asked for each boy's phone, and he studied them. Simon explained that he would be able to track each of their phones now, in case of an emergency.

The boys continued to discuss some of the more unusual points of Gabriel's day. The gentleman with the Mohawk was one topic that made Gabriel uneasy. Gabriel didn't have any real evidence, but the man did seem out of place. Also, Gabriel's dream couldn't be explained. Simon asked Gabriel to tell it once more, and they all discussed what it likely meant.

After some time, Gabriel looked at the time. It was almost midnight. The boys decided to call it a night. Tomorrow was Saturday, and the boys wanted to get some rest for their weekend. They agreed to meet tomorrow morning and address the situation with fresh, rested minds.

Gabriel left Simon's dorm room apartment, but Jake was already asleep on the couch when he left. Gabriel walked alone in the darkness back to the dorm. The campus seemed so much different at night. A few street lights illuminated the darkness along the path, but just a few feet from the sidewalk was complete and utter darkness. Gabriel would never admit it, but it was a little frightening.

His mind was still running at full speed. He was like a marathon runner trying to solve a jigsaw puzzle and complete math problems all at the same time. He felt as if he was trying to make all of these weird pieces fit, but to him they seemed completely impossible. Hundreds of possibilities rushed through his head. Even more questions raced through his brain than he thought there could be. Where was Serena? Who was the man with the Mohawk? Was Serena in danger? Could he just be overthinking things?

When he was about halfway home, Gabriel heard a noise; at least he thought it was halfway. He couldn't actually tell where he was exactly, but he was certain he'd heard a noise. It sounded almost animalistic, like a grunting beast from the forest near the school had gotten on campus.

He stopped to look around, checking the area in front of him. The path looked clear. Nothing was on the sidewalk at least. Then he looked behind him. There was nothing on the sidewalk behind him. Then he looked into the darkness.

However, he couldn't see a thing, and he had no idea from which direction the sound had originated. The dominating blackness was all consuming. It even seemed to swallow up the sound. Gabriel stepped off the path and looked into the open area before him. Still, he couldn't see anything.

Then he felt a pulling on his collar, and he was lifted up in the air. Two thick arms wrapped around him and held him so tight he couldn't move. He struggled as much as he could, flailing his arms and kicking his legs. Every time he connected with the body that was holding him, it felt like he was striking a steel wall. That's when Gabriel was hit with the most overpowering sense of déjà vu. He'd had this experience before, though he hadn't quite lived it—he had dreamed it. This was exactly how his dream went, though. In his dream, Serena was flailing against a massive human who was as thick as iron.

Gabriel attempted to push against the forceful arm impeding his breathing. However, he couldn't break the grip. It was like a titanium snake coiled around hi, squashing the life out of him. Just then he saw a hand in front of him. He noticed a smell for just a second, and then everything went black.

FILE #12

SOS

The room was blinding as Gabriel's eyes opened. Bright lights shown down from above, making it hard to see. He looked around and saw strange devices around him. It was hard to make them out as his vision was still blurry, his head foggy. When he tried to sit up, he noticed that he was strapped down by large buckles across his chest and legs.

His initial instinct was to panic, and he tried to struggle and force his way through the bonds that held him. As hard as he struggled, he knew he couldn't break them. He didn't know what they were made out of, but he could tell they were made to hold even the strongest person down. Then an idea came to him: using his gift, he could unbuckle the straps. So he focused on the buckled restraint and studied it for several seconds. In his mind, he envisioned it unsnapping and opening. He believed it would happen, and then he heard a click. He opened just his left eye and saw the strap over his chest fall loose.

Then he repeated the process on the second restraint, and he was free. He stood up and stretched. His muscles felt tight and rigid, as though he had been in that bed for longer than he realized. He looked around the room, trying to get a feel for the place he was being kept. It was a bright room, with blinding overhead lights. Empty hospital beds were all lined up in a row.

Gabriel hopped off of his bed and looked over to the far wall. There was a single door with a keypad, and there was a desk with a messy stack of papers covering every inch of it. After Gabriel rotated his head to look around, he realized how stiff his neck was. Gabriel stretched his neck and flexed his shoulders, trying to loosen his tension. Just as he started to feel his muscles relax, the door opened.

A man walked in wearing a dark charcoal suit. Instinctively, Gabriel hid behind the gurney. The man didn't seem to notice Gabriel when he entered. He was too busy furiously scarfing down a breakfast burrito. Then the man went to a stool at a desk in the far corner. He sat down and continued eating as he read some files he carried under his arm. Seeing an opportunity to escape, Gabriel crept to the door.

Gabriel made it to the door and stretched out his hand to open the doorknob. The screech of the handle turning was louder than he'd expected, and the man turned around, noticing the sound. The man stood, just about to yell something out. However, Gabriel held out his hand instinctively, and the man was sent flying backward. He flew over three of the beds and crashed into the fourth.

When he opened his eyes, Gabriel realized that he'd accidentally released a force of telekinetic energy that shot the man backward. Looking over the row of hospital beds, he saw that the man was on the floor, spread eagle and unconscious.

Gabriel was about to turn to the door when Gabriel thought for a moment. Instead of rushing out, he turned and ran to the unconscious man. He checked his pocket for a phone or a walkie-talkie. He found a cell phone in the man's jacket pocket, and he snatched it. It looked like a small, thin framed piece of glass. He pushed his hand against the screen, and it lit up. It worked.

Not waiting for the man to wake up, Gabriel bolted. The hallway was almost as bright as the room he'd exited. The floors were a bleached-white color, and the walls were bright white with chrome molding. It almost looked like a hospital wing.

He rounded a corner and saw a room with a sign that read Storage. Thinking this would be a safe place to hide, Gabriel darted over to the door. He ducked inside and looked at the man's device. Unlike the small, empty room he had been expecting, Gabriel was inside a massive storage room. There were large metal shelves that held huge wooden crates as big as Gabriel. He looked around and tried to understand all of the weird things he was seeing.

He rounded the corner of the first shelf and saw a row of boxes with the words "Homunculi Project" along the side. Gabriel mouthed the word to himself: *Homunculi.* Unsure of what he was seeing, he wondered what a homunculi was. It must be some sort of secret code for some part of whatever was going on here. That's usually how it worked in the movies. All the bad guys had secret names for their evil plans.

Realizing how dire his situation was, Gabriel snapped back to focus. He typed in a code word he knew only one person would see, "SIMON, OUR SAVIOR," and he hit Send.

In milliseconds, Simon's ears twitched, and his eyes shot from left to right. He sensed something, as if someone was screaming his name. He grabbed a small tablet on his desk and held it in his hand. He could see the message in his mind. Somehow he knew it was from Gabriel. He opened a channel that couldn't be hacked, and across the campus, the device in Gabriel's hands sprang to life.

Gabriel looked at the small device, and he could see Simon staring at him.

"Are you all right?" asked Simon.

"Simon, thank goodness," Gabriel said with excitement. "I need your help. I was kidnapped last night. I am in a building, but I don't know where. Can you help me?"

"Of course," answered Simon, an edge of worry in his voice. "I can track your position, and be there as soon as we can."

Immediately, Jake's voice rose over Simon's. "We will be right there, Gabe. We will help you out!"

***

As Simon put the phone down, Jake started rushing to the door. He'd overheard the whole conversation and was ready to act without hesitation. Jake looked back at Simon. Simon looked worried. Jake understood that look, but Jake was a man of action. There wasn't time to think or wonder about the situation; there was only action.

"You coming?" Jake asked.

Simon looked up. "Yeah, let me get my stuff together. You can wait for me downstairs."

Jake nodded and walked downstairs.

Simon held up his device and looked at it. A normal person could do so much with one of these devices, but in Simon's hands he could do anything. He could access any information he wanted from the Internet. His ability to communicate with technology allowed him to find things out that no other person could.

After a minute of deliberation, he pressed a quick succession of numbers on the device and waited. "Sir," he said when the voice answered. "Codename: Codex."

The voice on the other side of the line spoke. Simon listened intently for several seconds.

"Yes, he's gotten himself involved. Should we move to extract him?" Simon asked.

The voice on the other line stated something that confused Simon. "I am not a field agent, sir. I am in intelligence. I am not equipped to handle this."

The voice replied.

"Yes, I understand you need time, but ..."

After the other person spoke, Simon stood silent for a second. "All right, sir, I will. I have a friend; he will help me. I think he may be of some use."

Downstairs, Jake paced back and forth, his anticipation becoming unbearable. If Simon didn't come down in the next few seconds, Jake thought he would just leave Simon behind. But then he realized he had no idea how to get to Gabriel. So, he turned around and faced the door. Just then he saw Simon coming through the door.

"Oh, thank goodness!" Jake exclaimed. "Are you ready?"

Simon pulled out his device and showed it to him. "Yup."

"That's it?" Jake asked. "You had that the whole time."

Simon smirked and said, "True, but now I am ready."

Simon tracked Gabriel's location. He explained how he was doing so to Jake while they were running, but Jake barely understood a thing he was saying. A few minutes later, the boys found themselves in front of the building where Gabriel was being held. Simon used his device to track the location of the phone that Gabriel used to call him. Jake looked at the front. "It's the science lab," said Jake. "Gabriel's in there?"

"It seems Gabriel is part of an experiment," answered Simon.

Simon pressed his device and made some calculations in his head. "Hmm," he said. "All right, it seems that the building is clear of everyone except security officers. Except, huh, that's odd. There are some people inside that I cannot identify by their campus ID."

Looking over at his screen, Jake asked, "What do you mean?"

"The men inside, the ones keeping Gabriel, are not campus security or campus employees at all. They are not supposed to be here."

Just then Simon hacked into the security footage. He saw the men inside. He gasped in surprise. Jake looked at Simon's face.

"Do you know them?" Jake asked.

"Uh, no," Simon answered unconvincingly. "I was just surprised. They are probably gifted, though."

Simon walked up to the door and pressed his hand to it. As he stood there, Jake watched Simon mumbling something under his breath, but Jake couldn't hear him. It was as if Simon was talking to the door. Then it clicked open, and Simon turned the handle. They were inside just like that. As they entered, the boys were blinded by the sheer brightness of the building. Their eyes adjusted from the darkness outside.

Without much hesitation, Simon took point, looking around and gently feeling the wall, his fingers lightly tracing the smooth surfaces. The circuitry in the wall spoke to him. He heard it tell him there was an elevator. Simon walked down the hall, his hand sliding down the wall. Jake watched Simon as he slowly walked down the hall. Then all of a sudden, he stopped. Running his fingers up and down the wall, Simon checked the wall for something.

He lowered himself to the floor and pressed his tablet to his forehead. He muttered a few words that Jake couldn't interpret, but out of nowhere he heard a noise. At first it was a light humming, but then it quickly developed into the sounds of churning and cranking.

Simon looked toward Jake, a smirk on his face. Jake didn't know who this cocky kid was, but he was not the shy, inquisitive Simon he knew.

Simon opened his mouth, "I knew it—secret elevator. My readings tell me Gabriel is under the lab."

The boys entered the elevator. It closed, and Jake's heart started to pound. Now that the exit was cut off, the whole situation started becoming more and more real. Jake knew this wasn't just breaking the rules; this was big time. They weren't facing a slap on the wrist. This wasn't even as bad as being kicked out. Someone had kidnapped Gabriel, and if they could do that, who knew what they would do to Jake and Simon.

Within seconds the elevator opened back up. The sudden opening of the door made Jake flinch. Simon cocked his head toward Jake, looking at him out of the corner of his eyes. "When this is all over, things won't be the same, Jake. Gabriel just entered a world you can't even imagine. Hope you are ready."

Before Jake could reply, Simon moved out of the elevator. He rounded a corner and stopped at a door. The sign said Storage above it, and Simon opened the door. Gabriel was sitting on the floor with his hands held up ready to defend himself. Once Gabriel realized that it was Simon and not another goon come to take him, he stood up.

"I am so glad to see you guys. Thank you so much. I ... I don't know what to say to thank you guys."

Simon held up a hand. "Don't worry about it."

Jake still was stunned about Simon and the elevator, and his face showed his emotion. Gabriel noticed his concerned expression and asked, "Are you all right, Jake?"

"Oh, yeah. Of course, man. I'm just glad to see you."

That was when Simon interrupted them. "We need to get you out of here. Let's get back up the elevator and get out of this place."

The three of them moved to leave when Gabriel was struck with a sudden thought. It wasn't his thoughts. Flashes and images passed in his mind. A shadowy figure. A strange room. These weren't memories or thoughts. It was visions that someone was sending him. Then a voice clearly spoke to him.

"Gabriel, please help me. Find me before they make me do it," it said.

"Make you do what?" he asked the voice.

"If you don't come quickly, he is going to make me do something awful."

Gabriel looked up to his two friends and asked, "Did you hear that?"

Jake looked confused, and Simon was annoyed. Jake spoke first, sounding concerned. "Hear what?"

Through stutters, Gabe said, "It was Serena's voice. In my head. She was calling out to me. She is in trouble."

"What do you mean?" asked Jake.

Shaking his head as if trying to make it stop spinning, Gabriel answered, "Now it makes sense, all of the weird dreams and everything going on. It was her. She's been trying to communicate with me through her telepathy. Something has been, like, interfering with it. But I think we are closer now."

"She's here?" asked Jake.

Gabriel nodded. "Yes, she is here somewhere."

Simon tried to protest, but Gabriel wouldn't listen. He began walking in the opposite direction, when Simon yelled. "Gabriel, my orders are to get you out of here. I can't do that if you are going back into the lion's den."

Gabriel turned around and glared at Simon. He was not sure what he meant but he asked, "What do you mean by your orders?"

"I am an undercover agent, and right now my job is to protect you. Backup is supposed to be here soon, but we need to vacate the premises ASAP."

Gabriel's eyes narrowed. "If your mission is to keep me safe, then come with me and keep me safe. But I am not leaving my friend behind." Then he turned and continued to walk.

"You're going the wrong way, Gabe," Simon said.

Gabriel turned around and looked at the young man. He was pointing to the elevator. It was the only way to get to where Serena was. Simon knew how to find her and was the only one who could get them there. Gabriel knew it.

THE DOOR

When the elevator stopped, the boys exited one at a time, entering into a dark corridor. Large metal pipes ran along the ceiling and small strips of light lined the floor. Gabriel noticed how much like a sewer system the hall looked. It was cold, damp, and dark. The shadows clung to the walls, and although there were lights, they barely lit enough to see where they were going.

As the only one who knew where they were going, Simon led the way. He referred to his small handheld device every now and then. Gabriel wondered what it was like to speak to machines and have the ability to access all kinds of information as Simon could. It seemed like the coolest thing in the world to Gabriel. Without a doubt, Gabriel knew that Simon was very powerful.

The boys were about to round a corner, but Simon stopped them immediately. He held a hand out that stopped Gabriel. Jake bumped into Gabriel and stumbled back. Once again, Simon was communicating with his device. Gabriel tried to figure out what was happening.

"Why did we stop?" Gabriel asked.

Simon didn't answer right away. Maybe he was in too important of a conversation with his phone. Finally, he looked back and whispered to Gabriel. "There are some guards posted here. My device notified me just as they moved into the area."

"What are we going to do?" asked Gabriel. "Do you think we can take them?"

"Not likely. Neither of you are trained in combat, and my gift won't help me in a fight."

Instantly, Jake took offense. He was about to reply, but Simon stopped him. Simon added, "We may take them off guard, but they would overwhelm us in the end, Jake. We need to be smarter than they are. That is the only way we walk away from this alive. Got it?"

For the first time since Gabriel met Jake, he was speechless. Never before had Gabriel seen Jake unable to reply with some sort of comment or joke. Instead, Jake just rolled his eyes and said, "Fine. You're the boss."

"Now, I am having my device send a distress signal to these guards. This will force them to leave, and then we can easily slip past them," Simon said back.

Without much trouble, Simon's plan began. A signal was sent to the three guards who stood at the intersection of several tunnels. They looked at their devices and the woman in the group called for the two men to follow her. Within a minute, Simon got all of them to leave the area. Now they were free to continue without any obstacles.

The three boys came to the intersection with Gabriel now in the lead. He stopped at the exact spot the guards had been just moments ago. Looking down the tunnel they followed, Gabriel checked to make sure they were out of sight. Then he shot Simon and Jake a thumbs-up.

Simon waved them down another tunnel that looked just like the previous tunnel they'd trekked through. The low lights were dim, and it made the path difficult to see. The cold was only made worse by the dampness in the air. The pipes that ran along the ceiling and the walls dripped with moisture, making the air cold and wet. Every time Gabriel exhaled, he could see his breath in the air.

Finally, the path dead-ended at a massive metal door. Gabriel looked left and right to make sure there wasn't any other way to go. From floor to the ceiling stood a door that was a clean chrome. It looked like a massive elevator with a crease down the middle that separated the two halves of the entrance.

Just then Simon nodded at Jake. He motioned to the door, signaling for Jake to try and open it. It didn't take much prompting, not with Jake's macho attitude. He immediately rushed at the door. First, he tried to wedge his fingers in between the middle of the doors and pry it open. However, it was clear within seconds that it was not going to budge. Then Jake tried his gift. As he pressed his hand to the cool metal, Jake focused on his hand. He heated the fingertips and then snapped them against the door like a match striking a rough surface.

The small ember burned in Jake's hand. Realizing the potential danger, Jake looked back to Gabriel and Simon. He warned them to watch out. Gabriel and Simon took a few steps back and watched. In no time, the entire doorframe was engulfed in flames. The scorching embers roared out of control and surrounded Jake. In an instance, the fire rushed back toward Gabriel and Simon.

Gabriel realized the danger and, with a thought, created a protective barrier around Simon and himself. The roaring fires surrounded them on all sides. The small tunnel they were in wasn't a place to play with fire.

But just as soon as the fire came, it disappeared. Jake summoned the flames to himself, and they obeyed. He looked back at Gabe and Simon. "Sorry about that, guys."

"Yes, it would seem the pipes along the walls are releasing small traces of flammable gases. Fire was a dangerous choice," said Simon.

Jake looked back at the door. It was completely unharmed by Jake's flames. It didn't even appear to have heated up. In frustration, Jake kicked the door and walked away. "Your turn," he said, patting Gabriel on the shoulder.

Gabriel focused on the two different sides of the door. In his mind, he pictured them separating, and he saw the middle locking mechanism unlocking. Then he opened his eyes and tried to pull the two parts apart. Gabriel grunted and tried to force it open with his telekinesis. Despite all the effort, no amount of telekinetic power could get the door open.

"It's no use, man. It won't budge!" exclaimed Gabriel in exasperation.

Simon looked at the boys. "Just as I thought. It's an alchemic door. It has been designed by a master gifted with the ability to combine materials to create new materials."

"What do you mean?" asked Jake.

"Well, let's see. He could take a metal and a cloth and combine the two into a fabric that had the durability of a metal but the flexibility of a cloth. Understand?" Simon replied.

"I think so," answered Gabriel. "And he can do this with anything?"

"The alchemist I know can, but I don't know if he made this door or not."

Jake rolled his eyes. "That's all great and all, but how do we get inside?"

Simon smirked. "You two might be gifted with offensive abilities, but my power is this door's weakness. But I will need your help, Gabriel."

"How so?" asked Gabriel confused.

"These security systems can be difficult because they are programed to keep attackers out. So I need you to manually open the locks when I take down the system. Understand?" Simon asked.

"Not even a little bit," Gabriel answered honestly.

Simon looked at Gabriel and then at Jake and said, "When I tell you to, I want you two guys to force the door open."

"Can't you make the doors open with your gift?" asked Jake.

"I will try to convince the computer system controlling the door to open, but the system might be too advanced for me to beat it. If that is the case, I will try to distract it, and then you will be able to force the door open by hand."

Simon explained exactly what he wanted Gabriel to do. Then Simon focused on his device. His eyes changed from their normal color to a glowing green. He began speaking to the door's artificial intelligence, but the system refused to let him open the door. As Simon suspected, the system was advanced. It wouldn't allow him to simply open the door. Without a doubt, whoever had installed this system knew about Simon's ability. They'd devised a way to make this door as Simon-proof as possible.

With some quick thinking, Simon switched to plan B, deciding to distract the computer's system by making it think he wanted to upgrade the system. So, once he had the computer in a false sense of security, it would upgrade and then reset. While it reset, the boys would be able to open it manually. So as he got the system to reset, he motioned to Gabriel and Jake.

The boys crept up to the door, almost afraid that they would wake it up. They began pulling on opposite doors, Gabriel pulling left and Jake pulling right. At first, it seemed as if the door wouldn't budge. However, after a few good pulls, the doors seemed to slide. There was a loud clank flowed by the sound of churning gears, and then the doors slid apart.

When the doors were pulled completely apart, Simon and the boys rushed inside the gate as fast as they could. However, when they entered, they were terrified by what they saw. Inside the door, Serena was sitting on the ground with her hands covering her face.

She was crying and sobbing intensely. Gabriel couldn't understand what had happened. Simon rushed to her as Jake and Gabriel followed closely behind. They knelt to the ground, surrounding her. When she looked up, her eyes were red, and her cheeks were flushed. She had dark circles under her eyes. She seemed especially pale, and her hair was matted and frizzy.

"Are you all right, Serena?" asked Simon.

Gabriel looked at her intently thinking the same thing that Simon asked, only he spoke first.

She looked up and said, "I'm sorry. I couldn't help it. Please forgive me!"

FILE #14

SERENA'S SORROW

Just then Gabriel heard a sharp metallic ping in the distance. Gabriel hadn't noticed it before, but the room was very shadowy. The overhead lights were dim, and they were so high overhead that they didn't do too much to light the room. In the distance, Gabriel could see several large objects like machines and parts scattered around the room. Some seemed old and covered in dust, while others looked modern.

Serena was still crying her eyes out on the ground. Gabriel and Jake helped her up.

Simon looked around. "I don't like the looks of this place," he said. Something about this room gave him the chills. It had all the makings of a creepy horror movie: a cold chill in the air, a dark room, and crying in the background.

Jake and Gabriel didn't give him much attention. Both were concerned with their friend Serena. Immediately, Jake wrapped his arm around Serena's back and made himself a human crutch to help her up.

Gabriel looked at Serena, and he asked, "What happened, Serena?"

But just as he did so, they were interrupted by a man stepping out from the shadows. He coughed into his hands in a showy way as if he wanted to get their attention. The boys whirled to face the source of the cough. As they did, they could make out the shadowy figure of a man veiled in darkness. The figure moved out into the dim light. He wore a dark black lab coat that covered his tall, muscular body from his neck to his shins. His hair was long and just as black as his coat.

Although he seemed like the picture of health, something was odd about him. He was lean and had a picturesque physique. But what really startled everyone was his eyes. Gabriel didn't know how to describe it other than inhuman. The skin around his eyes had red spiral-like veins that looked like cracks.

"Yes, I know," the man said. "My eyes are a little unusual."

He grabbed a pair of goggles from a stand nearby and covered his eyes as he walked nearer to the group. "Better?" he asked, after placing them over his unsettling eyes.

"Who are you?" asked Gabriel.

Although Gabriel didn't know, Serena and Simon both knew exactly who this man was. Not only was he a colleague of Simon's, but Serena respected this man to no end. However, in his current state, Gabriel didn't recognize him. He looked like a stranger.

"Why don't you ask your friends, Gabriel Green?" said the man, finally stopping about ten feet from the group.

Gabriel, although confused as to how this man knew his name, was more baffled by who he was. So, Gabriel looked back and glanced at Simon and then Serena. He gave them a puzzled look like, *Who is this guy?*

Serena tried to speak through her tears, but she was unable to make a sentence. She was still so stricken with grief she couldn't even speak. So, Simon stepped forward and answered the questioning look.

"You know Dr. Drake, right?" asked Simon.

"Yeah," answered Gabriel. "I've heard him speak a few times."

"Well, this is him," Simon stated bluntly.

Gabriel was completely confused. The man before them was a full-grown adult, but he was nowhere near as old as Drake was. By the looks of it, Dr. Drake was in his late sixties maybe even his seventies. But this man was no older than thirties.

"How can that be?" asked Gabriel.

A soft, sobbing voice answered, "He made me use my telepathic powers to put his mind into a new body."

Gabe looked back at Serena.

Gabriel was about to ask a question, but she continued before he could. "He told me that if I didn't help him with his experiments, he would hurt me. But when I told him I couldn't, he threatened my friends. You guys."

Then Gabriel understood why they kidnapped him. It wasn't him that they wanted. He was just a tool to get Serena to do what Drake wanted.

Everyone was in complete shock. The idea that something like that was even possible was baffling even to Simon, who had experienced some very odd things in his young life. However, the most astonishing thing to Gabriel was the horrible act of threatening someone the way Dr. Drake had. This was beyond cruel; it was evil.

Gabriel turned back to face the man before them, this new Dr. Drake, as it were. He didn't see the man he admired for the work he did in the field of gifted research. Instead, he saw a man who would use the trust he'd received and then turn it against those who were willing to help.

Just then, Serena asked Drake a question in her tired voice. "Will you let us go now?" She paused, catching her breath. The ordeal of moving Drake's mind into a new body was so taxing on her body she was beyond tired. "I helped you get what you wanted. Please just let me friends go!"

Dr. Drake put his hand under his chin. He made a big show of thinking about her question. However, after several seconds he shook his head. "I am sorry, Serena, but I cannot let you go."

"Why not?" she asked, almost sounding as though she was about to fall asleep.

"If I let you go, then you will report to your superiors," he said, looking directly at Simon.

Simon's eyes widened. "How did you know?" asked Simon.

"You really thought I didn't know that you were a new agent of the Organization. I knew you were sent here to spy on me and report back to your superiors about my crimes."

Immediately all eyes turned to Simon. He smirked for a second, and then his smile faded. "Yup, you caught me."

Dr. Drake laughed at his prideful smirking. "Of course I knew. It was quite obvious that you were a spy. Your appearance on campus was too much of a coincidence."

"Is that why you had me moved me from the science lab?" Simon asked. "You suspected I was getting close to your research."

"I did move you because I didn't want you to interfere. However, none of my research would be in danger. All of it is right … up … here," Drake responded, tapping his head. He said each word slowly and intentionally. "So, there was no way of you finding it."

Once again Simon smirked. Dr. Drake sneered at his smile. Gabriel could tell that Drake was annoyed at Simon's expression. He must have hated how Simon's demeanor made him feel like he didn't have the upper hand.

Simon looked square into Drake's eyes. "You know with my gift I can still communicate with anyone using technology. Right?"

Dr. Drake smiled at his question. "I am fully aware of your gift, and I am fully aware of your limits. We are now so far underground that we are beyond the extent of your ability to communicate with anyone. You will not be able to signal for backup now, Simon Cruz."

Simon tried to sense the nearest communication with the ability to send a signal. Nothing around him had that ability.

Dr. Drake then said, "Try as much as you want, but none of the technology in this room will help you. I have made sure that none of it can broadcast a signal. Needless to say, you are trapped here."

Gabriel turned his head to see his friends in the corner of his eye. "We can still get out of here. He can't hold us here. Let's go!"

Dr. Drake tried to hold back a laugh, but he wasn't able to contain it. He looked up at the youthful teenagers and said, "You think you got here because of your gifts and your cunning, don't you?" Then with another laugh, he added, "You are only here because I allowed you to make it this far."

Gabriel looked to his friends, and he knew that they were in a terrible situation. Every second they spent here would be dangerous. Knowing full well they might have to force their way out, Gabriel had to think of something quick. There options were limited, but he had a plan. Well, at least it was a plan to make a plan.

Fortunately, for the group, Serena was a telepath. So Gabriel called to Serena in his mind. He hoped her mental abilities weren't so completely worn out that she could still hear him telepathically. Thankfully, she could. Gabriel told her his plan in a split second and asked her to relay the information to the group.

In no time at all, the plan was explained to everyone. Now was the time to act. Instantly, the kids ran in three different directions. Being the strongest of the group, Jake pulled Serena with him. He practically carried her around a large computer panel to their right and hid behind it. Likewise, Simon began running in a dead sprint as fast as he could to the opposite direction. Meanwhile, Gabriel rushed at Drake and threw up his telekinetic energy in a protective shield.

Despite his attempt, Gabriel was unable to stand up to Drake. Unknown to Gabriel, Dr. Drake was more powerful than Gabriel realized.

Just as Gabriel made his run, Drake punched through Gabriel's shield. Then Drake threw him over him with one hand. The weight of his body carried Gabriel through the air, and he landed in the shadows. Thankfully, he was able to soften the blow with his telekinesis but not by much.

Drake yelled out to the youths, "You think you can challenge me? I have made myself the ultimate being in the world. I have given myself many of the most powerful gifts I could find. I have more abilities than any other gifted in the world."

From the shadows, Simon answered back, "Yeah, but what good are those gifts if you can't find us?"

Then Drake realized what had just happened. While Gabriel had rushed him, the rest of the group hid in the shadows of the underground chamber. Now they were all hiding in the darkness, and Drake couldn't find them.

FILE #15

THE PERFECT BEING

Dr. Drake scanned the room. Although there were overhead lights, the room was poorly lit. Only small emergency lights were aglow on the ground, and the dimly powered lights were far and few between. And the lights that were powered weren't strong enough to light up the room. He knew that he wouldn't be able to find them by just looking for them.

Drake was a skilled gifted, just like Gabriel and Jake. He had a gift that allowed him to think about things at a high speed. Whereas a normal person could think of really only one thing at a time, Dr. Drake could process many things at once and be thinking about multiple things at once.

While he was scanning the room, he thought to himself. He thought about his experiments. Now he had a body that was as fast as his mind. His synthetic body was faster, stronger, and more durable than a human body. Fortunately, the telepathic girl had successfully transported his mind into the artificial body without complications. Well, except for the unusual side effect of his eyes, he was perfect.

This was not achieved by mere chance, thought to himself. It took countless experiments. It took scientific studies with volunteers, and when that didn't show results, he began experimenting on students. He even went so far as to have his underlings break into student's rooms and take blood samples from them. He even kidnapped some, like Serena.

All the while Drake was thinking of this, he was thinking of what to do with this current situation. In less than a second, he had an idea. He knew that looking for them would take too long, so he decided to scare them out. If he could make them move or have to think on their feet, they would make a mistake and he would have them.

With a loud voice, Drake called out, "I wonder which of you I will find first. It's only a matter of time now."

Drake held out his left hand, and it began to glow with a dark purple. He pointed his palm in the direction of a large machine, and when he focused, a massive arc like lightning surged forward and exploded the large device. As he suspected, someone was behind it. Jake and Serena were nearby. He could hear them moving in the shadows. He stepped toward the smoking remains of the large machine that he'd destroyed and peered over it. They weren't here, but he knew they had to be close.

He stepped around the machine to the spot he was certain they were hiding. After processing the paths they could have taken, Drake estimated that the odds were most definite that they had gone to the right and were hiding behind a barricade. So, just like before, he sent another blast of dark purple plasma energy in the direction of the students. It crashed through several massive machines and sent many of them flying through the air.

From a distance, Gabriel could hear the destruction happening. Panic began to take hold in him, and he knew he had to help. Drake began taunting them in the distance. Repeatedly, he made comments about how close he was to finding them and how they couldn't hide for long. Gabriel didn't know what to do. Then he had an idea. He could move things with his mind. Of course!

Across the room, Drake was approaching the spot that Jake and Serena were hiding. They ducked under a large shelving unit that had various small vials on it. Serena's breath began racing, but she tried to calm herself. Her panting was so loud she covered her mouth to stop the noise.

More so than Jake, Serena understood what Drake would do to them. She'd experienced the torment. Like forcing her to put his mind into that fake body, holding her against her will, threatening to destroy her family and her friends. The terror gripped her so tightly she could barely hold it in. Her heart was racing even faster than her breath.

Meanwhile, Jake was focusing on the sound of Drake's footsteps. He knew Drake was approaching because they steadily got louder and louder.

The sound of footsteps was just a few feet away when they heard a loud crash just beyond them. Jake and Serena's eyes both widened. Jake didn't understand, but whatever it was Drake's feet began moving past them into the direction of the noise. Jake and Serena took that opportunity to move further away from Drake.

Down a different path, Simon was hiding inside an overturned box he'd found. He fastened the lid and was trying his best to contact help. He knew they were so far underground that it would be practically impossible to get a signal to them through a device. Most technology was not designed to work under hundreds of feet of concrete, stone, and earth. He would have to do this himself.

First, he cleared everything else from his mind—all of the events of the day, the semester, and even the mission itself. He thought of one single thought. He focused on his supervising officer's phone in his office. He began thinking about what it looked like, and he focused on the frequency he would need to access it.

Try as he might, he just couldn't get the phone to ring. It was just too far away. Then he heard a loud smashing sound and a scream in the distance. He heard Drake's voice and a faint laugh. His eyes widened, and immediately he doubled his efforts to contact his officer. If Simon didn't contact him soon, they would all be in grave danger. He had to. Simon simply had to give him their location.

"Please work. Please work," Simon whispered to himself.

He focused harder and harder on the phone, trying to make it work. He knew he could do it. He had to do it. If he didn't Jake, Gabriel, and Serena would all be caught and worse. Just then he had a thought. Instead of trying to get and hold a connection to his officer's phone, maybe he could send a message.

So, he tried. He formed his thoughts into a message and pushed it into the small device on his officer's desk. He prayed as hard as he could it would get into the data stream of all the messages and make it to his phone.

Somewhere back on ground level, a small phone shook with three quick vibrations. It stopped, and the man with the dark skin and gray hair looked down at it. He wrapped his hands around it and read it.

It said, "Agent in distress. Require backup. Send now."

The man looked down and realized his device was protected by several layers of encryption. No one could access this device without the proper access codes. He didn't know how this message got through. He quickly typed back.

Just as he was about to start typing back, another message popped up. "Under science building."

In an instant, the officer was yelling into a satellite phone. His team of agents began to mobilize outside of the laboratory. Simon was hoping that his message got through and they would be sending troops to help them soon. He knew that they were in for it. Simon sighed with relief. Now even if they did get caught by Dr. Drake, agents would be here soon to apprehend him.

Over on the other part of the room, Gabriel moved in the shadows, approaching Dr. Drake. Gabriel could tell because of the way Drake was shuffling his feet as he walked. He was looking in the area of the noise Gabriel had made. Just as Drake approached Jake and Serena, Gabriel moved a machine several yards away from them. The loud screeching noise got Drake's attention, and he went to investigate the sound.

Now Drake began looking around the area for the source of the sound. His anger was rising. It became obvious to the teens when he began sending those massive purple blasts of energy, exploding the massive machines. From where Gabriel was hiding, he could see the flashes of light. For brief seconds, the room was lit with the glow of explosions. A small piece of debris landed just a few feet from where Gabriel kneeled.

Then Drake started shouting into the darkness. He must have realized that he'd been tricked, and he was not happy about it. Just then, Drake had a thought. It was his gift that allowed him to do this. He knew his ability, hypercognition, gave him the ability to use all of the gifts he wanted. So, since he had all of these gifts, why not show these youngsters all of them.

First, he threw up his hands, and Gabriel saw sparks of lightning dance off his fingertips. Then they rose higher and higher into the air. The stalks of lightning branched off one another until they hit the ceiling. Then the lights of the room brightened to well beyond their normal brightness. The room was suddenly brought to full light. As Drake looked down, he could see Serena, who was being aided by Jake, moving down a path of lined pallets with large stasis pods.

He moved down the aisle and lined himself up with them. The weakened Serena couldn't move fast. She was using Jake as a crutch. Drake's massive intelligence needed no gift to tell him that it was most wise to incapacitate the weakest first.

The doctor moved down the pathway with a quickness he had forgotten he had in his youth. This new body was more powerful than even his original young self. He had developed a formula from very specific experiments that gave him a way of replicating the gifts of specific students. He was pleased with the results. Now he would show these youngsters his power.

Quickly, Drake called on a gift he'd acquired but hadn't tried yet. Holding up his right hand, he sent a blizzard of icy wind at the ground around their feet. Instantly, the ground froze, covered in a sheet of ice. Not realizing what Drake had done, Jake and Serena continued to move, and they started to slide. Quickly, they lost their balance, first Jake and then Serena. Before they could get away, Drake was upon them.

Instantly, Jake's training in the sparring ring came to him. Coach V taught him what to do in situations where your opponent had the upper hand. As Drake stood over Jake and Serena, he held out his hand to grab her. Before Drake could make contact, Jake put his right hand in the water on the ground. He focused as best he could and superheated his hand. The water began to steam around his hand, causing a thick cloud of mist to surround them.

The steam covered them just as Drake began moving in toward Serena. It caused Drake to recoil and gave the kids just enough time. Seeing his moment, Serena slid backward toward Jake, and they moved out of range.

"Very clever," Drake called out. "I was expecting an offensive effort based on what I've learned about you."

Jake was about to answer back, but that would give away his position. It was all he could do to bite his tongue and keep Serena moving.

Meanwhile, Gabriel was rushing to meet up with them. But he didn't account for the fact that the room was well-lit now. As he rushed to his friends, he was hit by a burst of concussive force so strong that it knocked him off his feet. The impact of the shot was like hitting a brick wall. It hit him square in the chest, his feet lifted from the ground, and he slammed down on the uneven surface of a machine he was running past.

Holding his back in pain, Gabriel got back to his feet. He looked over and saw that Drake was staring at him. He was partially covered in a layer of fog. But Gabriel could see his eyes were glowing.

"Great, he can do that too. What else is new?" Gabriel said in a sarcastic tone.

Then Gabriel noticed Jake and Serena running in the opposite direction. The fog separated them and Drake, and Jake used the steam and fog to get away. Gabriel was impressed with Jake. He was playing smart. Maybe his training in the sparring team was really paying off, or maybe under all that bravado Jake was really wise after all.

Although Jake had momentarily evaded him, Drake wasn't worried. The room was sealed, and the teens literally had no way out. Drake would never let them out. Not alive anyway.

Drake turned and moved in the direction Jake and Serena had disappeared. He rushed down a parallel aisle, separated by a row of machines, broken computers, and other mismatched devices. All these parts served a purposed for Drake's upcoming schemes. But the most important matter was the situation at hand, dealing with these kids, harvesting their gifts, and extracting their abilities. Unfortunately, they had seen too much, and he couldn't release them as he had the other test subjects.

With tremendous agility, Drake jumped into the air. He leapt over the machines and, with a touch of one foot, was on the opposite side of them. He found himself just a few short feet away from Jake and Serena. As before, Drake knew he needed to incapacitate them but not with lethal force. He still needed Gabriel's and Serena in one piece.

With a powerful blast of energy, Drake sent several machines flying in every direction. In order to avoid the collision, Jake and Serena rounded a corner and sprinted to their right. But just like before, Drake sent another blast of red plasma energy. The explosion forced Jake to pull Serena to their left and rush down that aisle. This happened several more time until Jake and Serena realized that Drake had pinned them up against a wall. Several large machines blocked them from escaping to the left or right. Now Drake was hovering in the air in front of them.

Jake sneered at him. "Well, aren't you just full of tricks."

"You have no idea," answered Drake.

Drake landed before them. He had sparks of purplish-red lightning surrounding him. He was radiating some sort of pressure. It was as if the weight of his presence was crushing them. Jake felt as if he was going to be smashed under the impressive power that Dr. Drake possessed.

Just as Drake motioned to point at the youngsters, Gabriel rushed in front of them. He held his hands out in front of him and yelled, "*Stop!*"

Drake looked impressed. Drake thought that his previous concussive blast would have knocked Gabriel out of the fight entirely. Clearly, the boy had more willpower than expected. Regardless, Drake would not let this change his mind. With three of the four kids in front of him, Drake had most of the fish in one barrel. Now would be the time to act.

He decided to use some concussive attacks to weaken them and then capture them. So, he held out his hand and a powerful force of energy shot from his palms straight for Gabriel. The force was like a punch, strong enough to hurt but not kill. However, Gabriel was ready for it. He focused all of his energy. He envisioned a shield of telekinetic energy in front of him. The energy that Drake shot out at him just deflected off the shield.

Gabriel sighed when he realized he had done it. The hair on the back of his neck stood up on end. The excitement filled him with more determination. He smirked at Drake in a way that said, *Nice try.*

Drake was not amused by Gabriel's attitude. He decided it would not be a bad idea to put the young man in his place, show the boy now how powerless he really was. After all, Drake was taking it easy on him. He still needed the boy alive so he could extract his gift. But still, he didn't need to be completely conscious. Just as long as he was in one piece.

So, Drake amped up his attack. This time he used his ice. He sent a blast that was like an arctic wind at Gabriel. Icy shards of snow and freezing rain erupted in the air around him and shot at Gabriel. The force was so intense and the cold so biting that Gabriel winced in pain.

That biting cold. That sharp pain was something almost foreign to Gabriel. It was so powerful, so intense that it caused him to lose control of his gift for a moment. Instantly his protective field of telekinetic energy fell. He lost the shield that he'd created to protect his friends and himself. Without any prompting, he knew his mistake. He knew he was done for.

Gabriel braced himself for what he expected to be another attack from Drake's icy blast. Instinctively, he braced himself for the freezing chill, but instead Gabriel heard a snap and a burst of warm air. With eyes wide, he looked back and saw Jake standing before him. Gabriel's eyes moved from his face to his arm to his hand. From his hand was a roaring inferno. He had done it. Jake had generated a spark and created a flame. And he was using that flame to melt the icy attack from Drake.

For several seconds, Drake and Jake stood facing each other with their arms stretched out toward the other. Ice and snow flew from Drake's hands, and burning red flames leapt from Jake's fingers. Gabriel stood there watching in amazement. Jake was doing it—he was holding Drake back!

It was a strange sensation for Gabriel. The heat radiating from Jake's volcanic hands was so warming, but every so often, the artic like chill from Drake's gift sent a cutting child into the air that instantly caused Gabriel to shiver. Still, Drake's powerful icy attacks could not penetrate the flames that Jake was producing.

In just a few short seconds, Drake realized that going toe-to-toe with this young gifted would not win him this confrontation. So, instead, he decided to use his mind to outthink him. With his right hand, he continued to fill the air with his snowy attack, but with his left he used another gift. He summoned all of the moisture in the air around his left hand.

He smiled viciously. Never had another human used multiple gifts like this. He was the first. It was his gift that allowed him to do so in the first place. His ability gave him superhuman mental capabilities, which in turn allowed him to use all of these gifts simultaneously.

Then Drake shot a stream of water from his left hand. He curved the stream in an arcing pattern around the flames and directly into Jake. First, a plume of fog and steam poured off Jake's body. Steam wafted in the air from his heighted body temperature. Then, as more water sprayed him, his body temperature dropped to more normal. In just a few seconds, the inferno was extinguished.

Jake tried to snap again and again, but it was no use. Not only did the water make it hard to snap, but also his body was not heated enough to generate that initial spark. Before any of the youngsters could stop it, Drake sent another storm of ice and snow at them. Jake jumped in front of the blast, attempting to protect his friends. He was immediately sent rocketing backward into the wall. Gabriel heard him hit with a thunderous smack. Then his limp body slumped to the ground, leaving a large dent in the wall where his back had met the metal.

For a moment, Gabriel felt helpless. He and his friends had all tried and failed. He had never felt so helpless. Well, except for the day his sister was born. On that day, Gabriel couldn't do anything to help her. Then something started to burn inside Gabriel. Although he wasn't able to do anything to protect his sister, today he was. In this moment, he could fight to protect his friends. He knew he needed to do whatever was necessary to stop Drake. Gabriel would hold him off with ever last ounce of power he could muster.

Seeing his friend knocked back in such a barbaric, ferocious way caused a righteous anger to bubble up from the deepest part of Gabriel. His fury started to pour from his heart into his stomach, and he knew that he needed to do whatever was necessary to stop Drake. Jake had selflessly jumped in front of Drake's attack in order to protect him. Now Gabriel would do the same for his friends. Win or lose, Gabriel would hold him off with ever last ounce of power he could muster.

Drake exhaled deeply, firmly. Gabriel couldn't believe it, but he didn't even look fatigued. Drake yelled, in mock expression, "Round two!" Then he sent another wave of water. The force rocketed into Gabriel. He focused on the water and repelled them with his mind. Like before, he made a field of telekinetic energy by making the molecules of air denser.

Mentally, he prevented the water from passing him. However, he could feel the cold that caused the hair on the back of his neck to stand on end. It was surprising how much force the cold water had.

The pressure of the attack was getting stronger every second. Fortunately for Drake, there was so much moisture in the air, he could hold the attack almost indefinitely. All the water he shot into Gabriel's barrier would spray into the air. Then he could draw that moisture back to himself with his hydrokinesis, and then use it to attack again. He knew that Gabriel was young, and the main thing going for him was his youth. However, in time he would run out of steam and fall. This was the perfect attack to wait out Gabriel's gift.

After a few more minutes, Gabriel dropped to his knee. He was panting heavily. Drake noticed his change in posture and dropped his attack. Around him, a shallow pool of water covered the floor. Not only was there water all over the ground, but Gabriel felt his own forehead, and it was drenched in sweat.

Drake saw this as an admission of defeat. Threateningly, Drake held out his hand like he had before. Gabriel knew what it meant. Drake was readying another attack. Then, in his palm, Gabriel saw a small ember. Just a small flicker of light that grew into a small flame.

A shock ran through Gabriel. *What, fire too?* Then Gabriel saw Drake's maniacal grin. His evil smile sent a shiver through Gabriel. Then Gabriel's eyes widened. *Could it be? Could Drake have done it?*

"So, have you put it together, Gabriel?" Drake asked in a laughing tone.

"Did you steal that gift too?" Gabriel asked. "Does that mean you ..." He trailed off.

"Yes, it does Gabriel. Do you remember the day that you couldn't find your friend, Jake?"

"You didn't?" yelled Gabriel.

"I did!" answered Drake. "I kidnapped your friend." Drake's voice started rising louder and more intense.

Gabriel knew exactly when it must have happened—last semester when Jake was not in the hospital wing of the gymnasium. He had disappeared for several hours, and Gabriel had had no idea where he was. But now he knew where Jake had been.

Then Gabriel's eyes shot back toward Jake. He was on the ground, leaning up with Serena's help. She was making sure Jake was all right, keeping him conscious.

Drake smiled and said, "I didn't kidnap every one of the students I experimented on. For some, I just required a small sample of hair and that was enough. However, Jake's case was a unique one. So, I needed more time to study him."

Gabriel could feel his chest tighten. His heart race quickened. He felt the blood drain from his face, and his face was covered in sweat. Could it really be? He hadn't had an asthma attack in years.

His breathing was rapid but shallow. It was more like wheezing. On top of that, he could feel the stabbing pain of one of the headaches that accompanied his telekinetic gift. His vision was starting to grow fuzzy. His legs felt like jelly. His knees burned. There was almost nothing left in him.

Drake attacked once again with the flames that he threatened Gabriel with before. The flurry of embers rocketed at Gabriel. He had nothing left. He was running on empty. Gabriel was now on both knees. He knew that he couldn't hold a shield. He was barely able to breathe.

"Are you ready to admit defeat now, Gabriel?" Drake asked through a laugh.

But instead of answering, Gabriel held up both hands in a cross-shaped pose. He would not admit defeat. Instead, he showed Drake that he would sacrifice himself for his friends. Drake laughed as the flames grew closer.

FILE #16

SURVIVAL

Gabriel braced himself. He was expecting pain, unconsciousness, maybe even worse. There was a massive surge of energy and then a hissing sound like something sizzling. But instead nothing happened. He smelled the burning of ozone in the air. He blinked an eye and then looked up with hesitation. Instead of Drake, he saw a woman standing in front of him.

She was standing at an angle not facing Gabriel, but not really facing Drake either. Her hair was dark and long, stretching down her back. She wore a dark, dark gray suit. Gabriel could see black leather gloves on her hands. She was completely encased in an aqua-colored energy, almost like a suit of armor.

Drake threw a hand through the air to push away the smoke that was obscuring his vision. He saw the woman before him. He smiled as if he knew her. However, it wasn't a smirk that showed he was happy to see her. It was a face that said, *What are you doing here?*

Drake didn't know how she'd gotten into the room, but he knew that if she was here, more agents would be here shortly. This would change his plans. It was too soon to enact his plan, but if it came down to it, he would have to.

Just then Drake saw other agents jumped down from the ceiling. Instantly, Drake started piecing everything together. It might have taken another man several minutes to piece everything together, but Drake was no ordinary man. Immediately, he knew exactly how these agents had known to come—Simon. Somehow Simon had made contact with the outside world. It should have been impossible. The room they stood in was made of lead and surrounded in a thick layer of cement.

Just then Simon appeared. He looked at Drake with a cocky smile. The young boy was more advanced than Drake had expected. But even still, the ability to communicate with the outside through technology should have been impossible.

"Very impressive, Simon," Drake said in an even tone. He began levitating as the three agents who'd appeared from the ventilation shafts moved to reposition themselves. Drake looked beyond them to Simon. He wanted to end that young man. He wanted to make him pay for bringing his plans crashing down around him. He'd neglected to account for a gifted surpassing his supposed limitations. Somehow Simon had exceeded what should have been scientifically impossible.

Just then a large smashing sound reverberated through the room. Everyone stopped and all eyes turned to see the massive door that had barricaded them inside. The wall around it cracked in a pattern that looked like a spider's web. Then the walls fell apart like a curtain dropping on a play. All that was left were the massive doors.

As the last piece hit the ground, more men and women in suits were rushing into the room. It was like a small army of secret service agents. There appeared to be fifteen or twenty of them in the room, followed by a man in a white lab coat. The majority of them moved into position to surround Dr. Drake. Two others moved around to protect Simon. Gabriel wasn't sure why, but for some reason he was important. Then another stood beside the man in the white lab coat.

The man in the lab coat appeared to be in charge of whatever was happening here. The first thing Gabriel noticed when he was closer was his eyes. They looked like an interesting shade of silver, almost like chrome. However, his thick glasses were foggy from the warm, humid air. His shaggy dark hair was more gray than black at this point.

He was wearing a white button-down shirt with a red tie and black pants. Over that was his white lab coat. Unlike Drake's, whose lab coat was dark black and immaculately clean, this man's was very wrinkled and covered in burn marks and stains.

Once the man was completely in the room, he immediately made eye contact with Dr. Drake. He unbuttoned his coat and put his hands in his pants pockets. "Well, this is a fine mess you've made, Drake."

"Agent Duo, they would send my subordinate after me, wouldn't they?" Drake said in a scoffing tone.

"*Captain* Duo now," answered the man in the white lab coat. "You're being stripped of your seniority, and *I'm* being promoted."

Drake laughed a short quick exhale. "Congratulations are in order then, are they not?"

Duo lost his composure for a split second and yelled out, "This … this isn't how I wanted to move up in the Organization, Drake. I looked up to you, trusted you, and worst of all, I wanted to be like you."

Drake seemed shocked at Duo's rare show of emotion, but he immediately smiled. It was as if doing this to Duo brought pleasure to Drake, as if this wasn't an accident.

"I thought you and I were men of science. When we were given our gifts, were we not chosen to ascend the heavens and reach to be higher than the sun?"

Captain Duo looked back in disgust. "You can't be serious?" he asked. "You really believe you are some sort of god now?"

"Of course I am. My work is unprecedented, and I have discovered the key to giving myself more gifts. I am a perfect being."

Duo shook his head. "I can't believe this. What will Ein think?" he said under his breath. A small tear welled up in his eye, and he looked to the ground, trying to hide it. He paused for a moment to collect himself. When he first spoke, he paused to clear the lump in his throat. "Will you come in?" he asked. "Will you come quietly?"

The men and women that surrounded Drake were in a tight formation. Several of them moved in close, while others remained further back. Gabriel could tell that they were all gifted. Each of them had the distinguishing marker of a gifted. The unique eye colors.

Drake lowered his head and masked his face with a look of sadness. But when he looked back up a moment later, his face was no longer sad. Instead his expression was sinister.

Around Drake were a dozen or more agents in a semicircle pattern. They positioned themselves to keep Drake from using the main exit as well as to protect the students. There was a tension in the air as everything seemed to freeze around him.

Gabriel didn't think Drake was the type to surrender. He seemed to prideful, too arrogant.

But to Gabe's surprise, Drake assumed a posture of surrender. With a kneeling position and hands on the ground, he looked to be submitting. With both hands on the ground, Gabriel noticed a shimmer of light. It was the small deep purple as before. It sent cracks out through the ground that spread outward from his hands. Then the ground exploded.

Most of the agents were able to protect themselves when the attack occurred. One man was completely covered in gray and brown stones. Another girl used her own energy-based gift to screen herself with crimson energy. One flipped up and away with an acrobatic motion, and one more pushed back against the attack with her own blast of energy.

A few of the agents were unable to shield themselves from the attack. They flew backward into the air. For a second it seemed that Drake's attack had failed. He looked out at the crowd with a stunned look. Only two of the agents were remotely hurt by the attack. But just as quickly as Drake had attacked, Gabriel noticed his expression of shock morph into one of utter delight. It was like a child about to reveal a wonderful present to their parent. But the surprise Drake was about to reveal would only destroy.

He looked at three of the agents in quick succession. The first was a tall woman with very pale skin and stark white hair. The second was a stout man with dark brown skin and curly hair. The third was a tall man with thin features. He was the first to act. His body exploded in a tornado of dust and sand. Then the stout man pressed the ground, and just like Drake's attack, the ground started to crack and shake. In just a second a twenty-foot radius around him erupted into an explosion.

Whereas the agents were able to defend against Drake's attack, a secondary attack from behind was completely unexpected, especially since this attack was from their own allies. As soon as the explosion happened, there was a massive thunderclap that deafened everyone for a moment. Immediately after, the room was filled with a gray smoke that blinded everyone. From where Gabriel rested against the wall, he couldn't see any of the agents or Drake. With ringing ears, he thought he could make out the sound of banging and clattering from inside the plume of smoke.

Gabriel didn't understand. Why were the agents attacking each other? Gabriel didn't understand. Was this some sort of mind control? No, Drake had never acquired Serena's ability. So why? Gabriel looked for the woman with the green hair, but the smoke made it nearly impossible to see anything. Then he noticed the same aqua-colored energy inside the smoke. He knew that it was her. He saw a shimmering whip spinning around in the smoke cloud, and he knew that she was fighting someone.

Just then two more suited figures jumped into the fray from above. They were like blurs, and if Gabriel hadn't been looking in that direction already, he knew that he would have missed them. It wasn't long before they disappeared into the smog.

Gabriel noticed his hearing coming back to him. He was able to hear more acutely. The sound of boulders cracking against metal. The humming of energy. But before Gabriel was able to react, he noticed a swirling of dust and sand in front of him. Then the man who'd erupted into sand before reformed before him.

The tall, thin man was wearing a similar gray suit, with black gloves. Then he started moving toward Gabriel at a deliberate pace. Realizing the man was coming after him, Gabriel tried to summon his energy. But try as he might, the weakened youngster felt completely out of energy. He raised his hand, hoping to telekinetically hold his attacker, but Gabriel had no energy to speak of. Unfazed, the man continued to move toward him. Hoping he could will through the lack of energy, Gabriel tried to push him back using his telekinesis. Gabe barely noticed the man pause in his steps. Gabriel was completely out of energy. And to make things worse, things started to get fuzzy.

Just then he stopped. The man looked directly where Gabriel was, but his eyes started to widen. He looked left and then right. His face was wrinkled in confusion. "Where are you?" the agent screamed.

Unsure as to what was happening, Gabriel himself looked left and saw Serena hiding behind a piece of broken equipment. He noticed her focusing her left hand toward the agent who was intent on harming Gabriel, but then she raised a finger to her lips. Gabriel didn't understand how, but he got the idea. Serena was somehow hiding him using her gift.

Suddenly, the man rushed off in a different direction. Gabriel heard him yelling all sorts of expressions as if he'd seen Gabriel run in a random direction.

Before Gabriel could say anything, Serena slid on the ground beside him. She held her hand to his forehead. "You're burning up, Gabriel."

Not really paying attention to her concern, Gabriel asked, "How'd you do that?" His eyes were blinking as he was very dazed.

"With my gift, I can manipulate people's minds. I just made it so she didn't know he was seeing you." After her explanation, Serena tried to aid him, but there was nothing she could do.

The last thing Gabriel remembered before everything faded away was her begging him to stay with her.

Gabriel dreamed of a dark room. Inside was the thunderous clap of rocks smashing, orders being shouted from one to another, and then the din of explosions and people yelling in need of help. It was a dream Gabriel couldn't get away from. Try as he might, he couldn't do anything. Although his mind wanted to, and although he willed himself to move, it was as though he was trapped.

FILE #17

THE WHITE LIGHT

They say smell is the strongest sense tied to memory. When that clean chemical smell came to Gabriel, he thought of the hospital. He remembered the day his sister had been born and almost didn't make it, the feeling of not knowing if he was going to get to meet his sister. Even as a child, that fear had been real and terrifying.

When Gabriel's eyes flickered open, he heard a voice calling for someone. The first thing he noticed was the brightness. The room he was in was so ... so ... white. It was almost blinding. Even though he was groggy, Gabriel tried to sit up. Once his blurry eyes came into focus, he noticed the ringing turned into the beeping of machines. He looked over and saw the tubes that were connecting the medical machines to him, monitoring his vital signs.

Then a somewhat-familiar voice entered the room. It was the man from before, the man with the white lab coat. Try as he might, Gabe couldn't recall his name. His brain was bleary still, and everything from the past day or so was all jumbled up. Gabriel couldn't recall the name he'd heard in the laboratory, but he knew he recognized the man.

The man stood in the doorway, looked at Gabriel, and nodded, as if asking for permission to come into the room. Gabriel looked him in the eyes. When first Gabriel tried to speak, the words didn't come out. He tried once more to say something and realized his throat was so dry he could barely get a word out.

The man in the lab coat entered and stopped a few feet away. Gabriel noticed him grab a clear pitcher of water. He poured it into a small glass cup. Then he turned to Gabriel. With a hand held low, the man offered Gabriel the glass. At first, Gabriel wasn't sure if he should trust this man. He didn't really know him. However, as he thought about it, he realized that if this man had nefarious plans for him, Gabriel probably would have already been gone.

So, reluctantly, Gabriel took the glass from the man. He drank the water, and it was like a wave of refreshment poured over him. The water seemed to wash away the rust that had built over his mind. It was wonderful. He gulped it all down ravenously. With a gasp for air, he breathed in fresh air as if for the first time.

Gabriel leaned his head toward the man and asked, "What can I do for you, Mr. ... uh?" Gabriel paused to indicate he wanted the man's name.

The man replied, "Oh, right. You may call me Duo."

"What can I do for you, Duo?"

The man smirked. Gabriel could tell this man was not the serious type. However, he was in a situation of some importance, and he was trying to act serious. Then Duo said, "It is not the policy of my ... my organization to divulge this kind of information to a civilian. However, we have taken a special interest in you Galterio Green."

Gabriel made a groaning sound to interrupt him. "Please, call me Gabriel," he begged.

The man paused. "Fine, Gabriel," he stated. "Our organization was investigating the disappearances on the campus. We even had agents on campus. Some posed as professors, and others posed as students."

Then Duo paused and held a hand out toward the door. When the door swung open, Gabriel didn't quite understand what he was seeing. It was like seeing someone you knew when you were a child and then seeing them again later in life. They looked somewhat the same, but at the same time, you didn't really recognize them. This was exactly what Gabriel felt like when he saw the figure enter the room.

He was wearing one of those same two-button suits as the rest of the agents. His hair was slicked back, and he was wearing thick, black-framed glasses. It was Simon, but it wasn't the Simon that Gabriel knew.

"Hey, Gabriel," he said.

"Simon?" Gabriel begged as he lay in that bed. "What happened to you?"

"The thing is, Gabriel, I am an agent of the Organization as well. I was posing as a research assistant on campus as part of an undercover operation. Duo tasked me with scanning all of the online resources I could for anything that might help us find whoever was kidnapping these students."

"Why didn't you tell me?" Gabriel asked.

"That's really not something I could have. You see, if I leaked that I was an agent, all of my work would have been for nothing. Drake could have gotten away. Or have learned my identity and come after me." Then Simon paused. "I didn't want to hide this, Gabriel. But I was trying to protect you and all of the other students."

Gabriel felt silly, but at the same time, he knew that Simon was being honest. Simon was a good kid, and Gabriel appreciated his sincerity.

"So, what is this organization you two keep talking about?" Gabriel asked.

Simon didn't say a word. His eyes lowered to the floor. Then they rose and met with Captain Duo's eyes. He nodded to his superior. When Duo turned to Gabriel, he coughed into his hand.

"I am not really at liberty to say what our company does. However, you are aware of the Gifted Security Act? Right?" asked Duo.

Gabriel nodded. He had heard of this act in a class earlier that year. It allowed the creation of agencies with the expressed purpose of regulating and protecting the public from gifted individuals who would abuse their gifts.

"Our organization is one of the agencies. We work in undercover missions to take care of the public from dangerous and renegade gifteds. Without us, this world would be a much scarier place."

"I've heard of the Dawnstar Agency and the Cobalt Core. Are you one of those two agencies?" Gabriel asked.

"No, we are not affiliated with those agencies," Duo said.

Gabriel's head started to ache again. He rubbed his forehead. A layer of sweat coated his brow. It was cool, meaning it probably had been there for some time now. Simon stepped forward and looked concerned.

"Are you feeling any better?" Simon asked.

Gabriel nodded, saying, "I think so. My head is still a little fuzzy. I remember being in that room with Drake and you. But it's all a little jumbled."

Simon looked at Duo. The man pushed his glasses up with his forefinger and nodded. The second Simon's eyes focused back at Gabriel, he was spilling his secrets like it was the last thing he ever did.

"The operation was supposed to be a sting. We were moving in to apprehend Drake. We had enough evidence to bring him in on illegal experimentation and kidnapping charges. But when you and Jake decided to intervene, I had to contact my superiors. They moved in immediately. However, Drake somehow convinced some of our team members to betray us, and they helped him escape."

Gabriel sat up. "That's right," he said. "All of those guys in suits started attacking each other. Why would they do that?"

"We don't really know exactly. Maybe he bribed them. Maybe he blackmailed them. Who knows?" Simon added with a shrug. "All we know for sure is that they aided and abetted a criminal. That makes them as guilty as he is."

Captain Duo stepped up and with his hands crossed over his chest, he added, "So, Gabriel, to finish answering your question: after you passed out, Dr. Drake had one of his agents cover his escape with a light screen. We were unable to penetrate it, and we couldn't get through the metal plating quick enough to burrow under it. So, unfortunately, Drake escaped."

Captain Duo's eyes narrowed as he spoke. His demeanor become more and more stern as he continued.

"We have teams out searching for him, but we don't have any leads just yet. We hope to scan the rest of his lab for information."

Simon's posture dropped. A look of confusion and anger covered his face. His eyes were glassy as Gabriel looked at him. Simon sat down on the hospital bed's edge near Gabriel's feet. His hand was holding the handle at the foot of the bed, and Gabriel could see he was holding it so tight he might break it. Finally, he spoke what was on his mind. "Drake ruined everything with his God complex. No, his gifted complex."

Duo nodded. He then unfolded his arms and wheeled around the opposite side of the bed as Simon. He stopped and looked at Gabriel. "That brings us to our last point."

Gabriel looked up with a raised eyebrow. "What's that?" he asked.

"It seems Drake's plan may have been a large-scale operation on his part. Several of our teams and safe houses around the world were attacked by agents who were supposed to be on our side. We estimate about one-third of our agents have betrayed us."

There was a pause for a moment. Then his expression changed. He seemed to force a smile and added, "So it seems we have some job openings. Do you think you would be interested in helping out our team?" Duo asked with a somewhat upbeat tone of voice.

Gabriel looked shocked for a moment. "You mean like one of those agents?"

Duo laughed a deep, hardy laugh. "Yes, like one of those agents."

"Why me?" Gabe asked.

"Well, we are a secret agency, and for better or worse, you know of our existence. So, we think we could enter into a mutually beneficial agreement. We train you, and in turn you work for us in apprehending potentially dangerous gifteds."

"How ... no ... *where* do I begin?"

"You will receive training and a mentor who will oversee your training."

"Who will that be?" asked Gabriel.

"We have someone on campus already, a 'recruiter' of sorts for us," Duo said while making air quotes with his fingers. "They will take on the role of your mentor. Is that all right with you?"

"Of course, I definitely want to help. It's always been my dream to do something to help out and protect my family. You can count me in," Gabriel said and held out his hand.

Duo grabbed Gabriel's hand and shook it. It was a tight, firm grip. He didn't crush his hand, but it was firm enough to let Gabriel know this was a man who had some authority.

"Excellent, Gabriel. We look forward to working with you. We will keep Simon on campus for a while longer. He has some more work to do, and we want to make sure he has a nice space to do it," Duo looked over to Simon.

Simon nodded, and Duo turned around to leave. Gabriel didn't understand his meaning. What work did Simon still have to do? Likewise, Simon stood up and headed for the door. He moved at a quick pace to keep up with Duo. "Your friends are in the next room. They are very anxious to see you. Want me to send them in?" asked Duo.

"Yes, thank you," Gabriel said emphatically. He was so caught up in the conversation he almost forgot about Jake and Serena.

Within moments, the two of them barged into the room with a flurry of cheers. They each surrounded Gabriel and sat on opposite sides of Gabriel's hospital bed. Jake had a bandage over his head, and Serena still looked extremely pale. But regardless of their physical state, for a moment they were completely ecstatic to see each other.

Jake nudged Gabriel when he sat down. "Serena tells me you saved her. Both of us really."

Gabriel smiled, but then his face grew red. He was overcome with a sudden heat on his face. It felt as if his face could be melting.

Just then Serena pinched him. Gabriel winced and recoiled. "Ow," he yelled. "What was that for."

Serena smirked in that signature way she did. "Just making sure you're real."

"What, of course I'm real."

"Thank you for helping me, Gabriel," she said. "Both of you. All of you."

Very matter-of-factly, Gabriel answered, "We are even. You saved me too back there."

Serena nodded.

"You're our friend, Serena," Gabriel said, still rubbing the spot on his upper arm where she pinched him. "Friends look out for each other."

She smiled and her freckles became even more red. In fact, her whole face blushed a little red.

"Thank you," she said. "I don't think I've ever had friends like you before."

"Well, you do now," said Jake. "But what do you think happened to Dr. Drake?"

"I think he escaped. That's what Captain Duo said anyway," Gabriel answered.

Jake was quiet for a moment, looking contemplatively.

Just then Simon came back to the room. He was once again dressed in his usual clothes; he wore a shirt with a planet on the front and jeans with sneakers. He told the rest of them that Gabriel was free to leave and that he wanted to escort them back to his dorm room. So, the group gathered themselves and returned to Gabriel's dorm room. Simon and the rest spent the day just lounging and enjoying each other's company.

They tried their best to forget the events of the evening, but with so much that had happened, Gabriel kept finding himself wondering what was going to happen next. Would Drake return for revenge? Would he come back for Serena? And would Gabriel really be a good agent?

He had no answers but hundreds of questions. Every now and then, Simon noticed Gabriel's expression. He knew exactly what Gabriel was thinking. He'd had the same thought when he'd received this mission, so many questions of what would happen. But for all of his questions, there weren't any answers.

Simon thought back to the phone call he received right before he went back in to see Gabriel and the gang.

He stood in the hallway near an office. He had just changed into his other outfit, the clothes he called his costume because they were the things he wore to keep up his cover.

As he stood in the room, his phone buzzed in his pocket. Immediately, he retrieved the small glass-like gadget and answered it. On the other end a voice asked him, "Agent Codex?"

"Yes, sir. It's me."

"Good," the voice said. "I want you to keep an eye on Gabriel Green and his friends. They could be in danger, and we want to keep them safe for the time being."

"Understood, sir," Simon said as the voice ended the call.

Simon returned from his memory as Jake made some joke that he missed. Simon smirked and made a fake chuckling sound to blend into the conversation.

EPILOGUE

The doctor coughed into his hand. The air in the hallway was thick and damp. These old basements were nothing like his clean, almost sterile laboratories. There was a scent in the basement, like that of old, stagnant water.

The figure that he followed didn't speak. He couldn't even tell if it was male or female because of the mask and long robes. However, he followed quietly all the same. Moments like these were always the hardest for Dr. Drake. More so for him than a normal person. The sheer speed of his mental capacity meant he went through thousands of scenarios in his mind. *Was he about to be scorned? Would his benefactors fire him? Or would it be worse?*

Every scenario played through his mind over and over again. A normal mind wouldn't have the time to process so much so quickly. But his brilliant mind did. In these moments, it was more of a curse than a blessing.

Finally, the person in the mask stopped and opened a door for him He stepped into the dark room. There was a large table with several silhouetted people seated around it. All of them wore masks or headdresses to hide their identities.

"We have arrived," he said to the dark room. The individuals poised around the large table all sat in complete silence. He stepped further into the room.

When no one answered, Dr. Drake shifted slightly. "Shall I return to my quarters?"

"No," answered a voice from across the table. "We still need to talk."

"What about?" Drake asked, a slight catch in his throat.

"The next phase of the plan."

"And what is that?" Drake asked.

"You don't need to worry about that," a male voice replied. "But we need you to continue your good work, doctor."

"Although I left most of my research back at the lab, we're in luck that my gift allows me to store it all up here," Dr. Drake said, pointing to his head.

"Very good," replied a feminine voice.

ABOUT THE AUTHOR

L. D. Valencia has always loved telling stories. It wasn't until he started his Master's Degree that he was convinced by a student to take his ideas to the published world. He currently lives in the Nashville area with his lovely wife. He hopes to inspire his students to love reading and writing. This book is a testament to that dream. Education is his goal, reading is his passion, and writing is his dream

Made in the USA
Monee, IL
24 August 2020

39544142R00100